Praise for Tim Myers's Candlemaking Mysteries

Death Waxed Over

"Excellent storytelling that makes for a good reading experience . . . [Myers] is a talented writer who deserves to hit the bestseller lists." —*The Best Reviews*

Snuffed Out

"A sure winner." —Carolyn Hart, author of the Death on Demand Mysteries

"An interesting mystery, a large cast of characters, and an engaging amateur sleuth make this series a winner." —*The Romance Reader's Connection* (four daggers)

At Wick's End

"A smashing, successful debut." —*Midwest Book Review*

"I greatly enjoyed this terrific mystery. The main character . . . will make you laugh. Don't miss this thrilling read." —*Rendezvous*

"A clever and well-done debut." —MysteryLovers.com

continued . . .

Praise for Tim Myers's Lighthouse Mysteries

A MOLD
FOR MURDER

TIM MYERS

BERKLEY PRIME CRIME, NEW YORK

THE BERKLEY PUBLISHING GROUP
Published by the Penguin Group
Penguin Group (USA) Inc.
375 Hudson Street, New York, New York 10014, USA
Penguin Group (Canada), 90 Eglinton Avenue East, Suite 700, Toronto, Ontario M4P 2Y3, Canada
(a division of Pearson Penguin Canada Inc.)
Penguin Books Ltd., 80 Strand, London WC2R 0RL, England
Penguin Group Ireland, 25 St. Stephen's Green, Dublin 2, Ireland (a division of Penguin Books Ltd.)
Penguin Group (Australia), 250 Camberwell Road, Camberwell, Victoria 3124, Australia
(a division of Pearson Australia Group Pty. Ltd.)
Penguin Books India Pvt. Ltd., 11 Community Centre, Panchsheel Park, New Delhi—110 017, India
Penguin Group (NZ), 67 Apollo Drive, Mairangi Bay, Auckland 1311, New Zealand
(a division of Pearson New Zealand Ltd.)
Penguin Books (South Africa) (Pty.) Ltd., 24 Sturdee Avenue, Rosebank, Johannesburg 2196,
South Africa

Penguin Books Ltd., Registered Offices: 80 Strand, London WC2R 0RL, England

This is a work of fiction. Names, characters, places, and incidents either are the product of the author's imagination or are used fictitiously, and any resemblance to actual persons, living or dead, business establishments, events, or locales is entirely coincidental. The publisher does not have any control over and does not assume any responsibility for author or third-party websites or their content.

PUBLISHER'S NOTE: The recipes contained in this book are to be followed exactly as written. The publisher is not responsible for your specific health or allergy needs that may require medical supervision. The publisher is not responsible for any adverse reactions to the recipes contained in this book.

A MOLD FOR MURDER

A Berkley Prime Crime Book / published by arrangement with the author

PRINTING HISTORY
Berkley Prime Crime mass-market edition / April 2007

Copyright © 2007 by Tim Myers.
Cover art by Mary Ann Lasher.
Cover design by Annette Fiore.
Interior text design by Kristin del Rosario.

ISBN: 978-0-425-21487-9

BERKLEY® PRIME CRIME
Berkley Prime Crime Books are published by The Berkley Publishing Group,
a division of Penguin Group (USA) Inc.,
375 Hudson Street, New York, New York 10014.
The name BERKLEY PRIME CRIME and the BERKLEY PRIME CRIME design are trademarks belonging to Penguin Group (USA) Inc.

PRINTED IN THE UNITED STATES OF AMERICA

10 9 8 7 6 5 4 3 2 1

To Patty and Emily,
for all the reasons there are,
and to every reader
who has enjoyed visiting
Elkton Falls, Micah's Ridge,
and Harper's Landing.

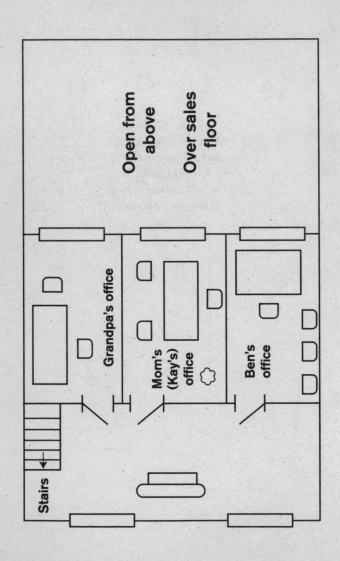

Open from above

Over sales floor

Grandpa's office

Mom's (Kay's) office

Ben's office

Stairs

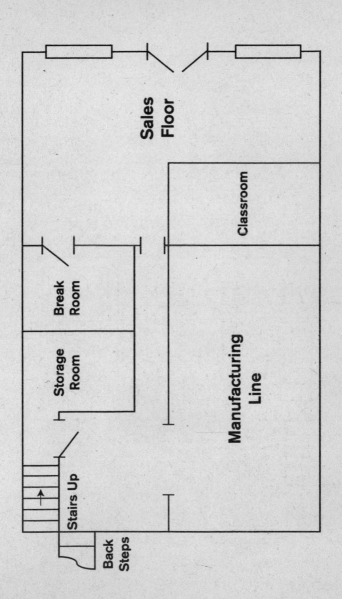

ONE

. . .

IN a way, I suppose you could argue that the murder was my fault.

After all, I'm the one who came up with the idea of hosting the Soap Celebration at my family's soap boutique and custom soap manufacturing production business.

Where There's Soap is the adhesive that holds my family together. My three sisters work in the front boutique and teach most of our custom soapmaking classes, while my three brothers operate the production line in back. My mother oversees the entire business, and my grandfather takes a turn at advertising now and then, though he was in Europe at the moment of the homicide. I envied him the ability to come and go as he pleased, but with my responsibilities, there isn't much time for travel.

I am the family and business troubleshooter.

My name's Benjamin Perkins, and there are more times than not that I would have traded with any of my family

members for a job with well-defined duties and responsibilities. Not that I don't keep busy. I like to help out wher-
ever I can—whether it is teaching a class of my own up
front or helping my brothers in back—but usually there is
something urgent that needs my attention.

I'd come up with the idea for the Soap Celebration as
a way of adding some normalcy to my professional life.

And then it backfired on me, and I had a murder to deal
with instead.

SHE swept into the soap shop an hour before I'd been expecting her, wearing a regal shade of red, from her gloved
hands to her dress to her shoes. At first, I didn't recognize
Contessa New Berne from the glamorous photograph her
publisher used on the backs of her crafting books. The
photos had to have been at least twenty years old, and even
then, they had obviously been retouched by an expert. Also
in my defense, some of her features were hidden by a
floppy hat in the pictures, and I wondered if she thought it
made her look fashionable, or mysterious, or maybe she
was just inordinately fond of headwear. At least she wasn't
wearing one now, though the rest of her outfit was identical
to the one in the photograph. It was like an odd portrait of
Dorian Gray, the woman changing but the outfit staying the
same over the years.

The contessa, as she liked to be called—so her personal
assistant, Sharon Goldsmith, had informed me frostily—
was the reigning queen of soapmaking how-to books, and
it had been a real coup arranging for her visit to our festival. She'd even waived some of her usual speaking fees
when I'd choked on the amount they'd asked for. For some
reason, I had been under the mistaken impression she

wanted to visit Harper's Landing and our little shop, but that was before she actually arrived.

She strolled up to me, scowling as she passed the stacks of her books for sale and the worktable prepared for her talk and demonstration later.

"I was told you are Benjamin Perkins."

"I am indeed," I admitted. "Are you here for the talk?"

She looked quizzically at me. "How else on earth could you host it if I weren't? I am Contessa New Berne." She offered a gloved hand to me, and I took it after a moment's hesitation. Upon closer examination, I could see that her glossy brown hair was a shade not found in nature, and not even an industrial-strength girdle could hide the extra pounds she was sporting. I wanted to ask for a photo ID, but after staring hard at her, I could finally make out the resemblance between the woman standing before me and the one on the publicity posters in the shop.

"It's nice to meet you," I said, trying to recover as graciously as I could. "I wasn't expecting you this early."

She withdrew her hand and waved it in the air like a conductor's baton. "The bed-and-breakfast where I'm staying is absolutely dreadful. Surely you could have done better than that hovel for my visit."

I knew for a fact that Jean Henshaw ran the second nicest place in Harper's Landing, North Carolina, and the swankiest accommodations we could afford. I'd wanted to put the contessa up in one of the more moderately priced hotels on the outskirts of town, but her assistant, Sharon, had refused the request, demanding the ultimate elegance we had to offer for her employer. If the price was any indication, Jean's place was indeed one of the best our area had to offer. I'd been coerced into providing two rooms for three nights, though the contessa would only be appearing at our store for one afternoon. Sharon had curtly informed me that the contessa never traveled without her, and that I needed to find proper accommodations for them both. As to the additional nights, since travel was so wearying for the writer, it was explained to me, she needed time to acclimate to her new surroundings, then to unwind after the event before jetting off to her next appearance.

As things stood, we were going to have to sell a ton of soapmaking supplies to recoup our investment, and I was hoping the woman was worth it.

"I'm sorry you're unhappy," I said. "I'd be glad to personally move you out to the Mountain Lake Motel if you'd like." The Mountain Lake wasn't exactly a dump, but it couldn't touch Jean's accommodations.

"I don't think so," she said with one raised eyebrow. "I understand the Lakefront might be more to my liking, though."

There was no way on earth we could afford a place as elegant as the Lakefront Inn, but I couldn't come out and say it so baldly. "We tried, but they were booked solid. Sorry."

"Very well," she said with a sigh, as if her graciousness alone was all that was keeping her there. "Now, Ben, I need your help. I must have some time alone before I speak. Is there someplace I could get away from my fans in order to focus my energies on my presentation?"

I looked around, and if anyone shopping in the store had noticed her, they were doing a fabulous job of disguising their delight. Still, she was the main draw for our event schedule, so it couldn't hurt to make her happy, especially since it wasn't costing me anything. "Of course. We have a break room that you'll find comfortable, and it has the added bonus of being stocked with some of the best baked treats in this part of North Carolina."

"Where is it?" she asked.

I pointed to the door toward the back, just off the selling floor where we were standing.

She frowned at it in disdain, then asked, "Don't you have anything more . . . private?"

"I suppose you could use my office," I said. "It's upstairs, and it has a beautiful view of the shop down here." I gestured to the darkened glass above us.

"There's an elevator, I presume," she said.

"No, ma'am, but the steps aren't bad."

It was clear that I'd somehow managed to disappoint her yet again. If this woman put on her high-and-mighty act during her presentation, I was going to have people throwing bars of soap at her to get her off the stage.

"Very well," she finally agreed. "Lead the way."

I led her through the hallway door to the back, past the idle production equipment and up the stairs. My brothers had howled when I'd demanded they shut the line down for the two days of festivities, but Mom had backed me up. We needed their help out front, and whether they liked it or not, they were going to be working the cash registers later, hopefully until their fingers were bruised from ringing up all of the sales we were going to make.

I led the contessa into my office, and she looked around with a critical eye. I could swear I saw her deliberately sniff the air before she turned to me and said, "As green rooms go, this is rather squalid."

"As an office though, I like it just fine." I was half expecting her to ask for a basket of red M&M's and a Swedish masseur, but she plopped down in my chair and immediately swung around to survey the sales floor below.

"I'm concerned about something," she said as she tapped the glass. "Are you certain you have enough books?"

"I think we'll be fine." I'd pushed Mom to order the contessa's books through Diana Long, my current girl-friend and the woman who also happened to own the only independent bookstore in town. Though Dying To Read carried mysteries exclusively, Diana had used her re-sources to order the books for our event. She'd be handling the autograph session after the contessa's presentation since she was used to dealing with authors and we weren't. While Diana had told me that most of the writers she hosted at her shop were delightful, she had shared enough horror stories to make me realize that she'd be our best choice for han-dling the contessa. I scanned the crowd of shoppers below and saw that she'd slipped in since I'd escorted our guest upstairs.

"Is there anything else you need?"

She waved that gloved hand at me again. "No, you may go. I trust you've set up my materials as requested?"

Demanded would have been a better choice of words. The contessa's assistant, Sharon, had dropped by the shop the night before with a diagram in her hand, every detail spelled out. It had taken me half the night to get it just right, and Sharon had stayed until past midnight to make sure of it.

"Will your assistant be joining you soon?" I asked.

"Sharon will introduce me, of course, but beyond that, I'm not quite sure what the girl is up to. If I didn't know better, I'd swear she was sleeping in. Her door was closed when I left this morning. Now if you'll leave me, I must focus on the presentation ahead."

"Glad to," I said as I scooted out the door. I thought about putting a DO NOT DISTURB sign up on my door, but nobody had any reason to come up there. Mom had the only other active office upstairs since my grandfather had deserted his, and she was fluttering around the sales floor below like a butterfly searching for a place to land.

I was at the bottom step when I found myself wrapped in the embrace of a solid, curvy brunette with deep brown eyes. After Diana kissed me, I said, "I'm happy to see you, too."

She laughed, a sound that never failed to delight me. I'd been recently dumped in a budding relationship with Kelly Sheer—a local attorney now trying to reconcile with her ex-husband—when Diana and I started dating. It had been tough going at first, but it hadn't taken long for her to capture a very special place in my heart.

"You must be excited," Diana said. "There's quite a crowd out here already."

"I just hope our guest of honor doesn't disappoint them," I said.

"What's the matter, do you have a diva on your hands?"

"Diana, she showed up wearing red satin gloves; this from a woman who makes soap. You'd think she produces gold in that kitchen of hers instead of cleansers."

"Her books are popular, Ben," Diana said. "I've asked some other independent sellers I know, and they say she moves a lot of books for them. Besides, she probably wears the evening gloves to keep that 'glamour' image she tries to portray." Diana lowered her voice as she added, "She's not really a contessa, you know, or any kind of royalty at all. The entire getup is an elaborate pseudonym for her writing persona."

"So what's her real name?" I asked. If the self-proclaimed contessa got too pretentious, I'd drop her real moniker casually into the conversation just to get her attention.

Diana frowned. "I don't know. I did some snooping

around on the Internet after I ordered her books, but it's a pretty closely guarded secret."

"Isn't that the whole point of a pseudonym?" I asked.

"You're kidding, right? Mystery writers use them all the time. I even know one man who's got another series that he writes under a woman's name."

"How did that happen?" It truly was a fascinating business she worked in, and sometimes I thought she had the better career between the two of us.

"He came here for a signing once and I asked him the exact same thing. It turns out that a different publisher liked his style, but they thought he'd sell more books with a female name because of the traditional mysteries he writes."

"And were they right?"

Diana grinned. "I don't know yet, it's too early to say, but I like everything he writes."

Cindy, my youngest sibling, poked her head through the door. "There you are. Ben, Mom's looking for you. Should I tell her you're canoodling in back with your girlfriend?"

I was starting to answer when Diana beat me to it. "In all honesty, I wanted to canoodle, but Ben said he was too busy so I'm settling for a little gossip instead."

Cindy smiled. "Oh, goody. I adore dirt. Tell me."

I brushed past her and said, "I'd love to, but you said it yourself. Mom needs me."

She stuck her tongue out at me—something that made her look barely as old as the eighteen years she had—and Diana trailed along behind.

"Spoilsport," Cindy said.

"Every chance I get," I replied.

Once we were out on the sales floor, Diana said, "I'd better make sure the books are in their proper sequence of

publication. Sharon was pretty emphatic about it when she
came by the bookstore yesterday afternoon."

"So she read the riot act to you, too?"

Diana smiled. "She's nice enough, but I get the distinct
impression she isn't her boss's biggest fan."

"I can't imagine that," I said with a smile.

"See you later," Diana said as she moved to the table
stacked high with the contessa's books.

I found Mom by the front register, and from the pained
expression on her face, I had a feeling that I was going to
have more trouble on my hands than a temperamental
writer. My mother was a slim woman with frosted hair, and
it always delighted her when people expressed shock at the
fact that she had seven children, the youngest already
eighteen.

"I've seen that look before," I said as I neared my
mother. "What's wrong?"

"Benjamin, I know I should be happy we're filling up,
but there are too many people here. Perhaps we should
have gotten more help for these events."

"Don't worry, we've got it under control," I said. "With
the guys helping out up front, we should be fine." I patted
her shoulder as I added, "Enjoy it, Mom. It's a day to celebrate."

The frown left her mouth. "Yes, of course you're right."
She gestured all around us, then added, "It was a wonderful
idea, Benjamin."

"Thanks," I said as I watched a little old man try to
shove a selection of soaps under his coat. "I'll talk to you
in a second. I've got to take care of something."

I left her and caught up with the thief just as he stepped
outside our front door.

"Can I help you?" I asked as I touched his shoulder.

He acted as if I'd shot him. The man spun around out of my grasp, ejecting stolen soaps from under his coat like they were on fire. My grip loosened for a second, I was so startled by the display, and he managed to slip out of my grasp. The man must have been a sprinter in younger days, because he bolted off the porch so fast that he was gone before I could catch my breath. I collected the errant soaps and walked back inside. I'd been hoping no one had caught the exchange, but of course my mother had seen it all. She motioned to me, and I walked back to her, prepared for a scolding.

Instead, she hugged me. "Nicely done, Ben. I believe you are in control after all."

I just shook my head, then I started trolling through the crowd more earnestly, trying to spot anyone else who wanted to help themselves to our handcrafted products. It suddenly occurred to me that my office would be the perfect place to spot miscreants, but unfortunately it was occupied at the moment. That still left my grandfather's and mother's offices open, though. But I needed someone on the ground to nab any culprits I found, and unfortunately, my entire family was busy at the moment helping legitimate customers. I did the best I could acting as the entire store security team, but I wasn't sure if it was enough on a day like we were having. Who knows how much inventory walked out without the benefit of a receipt? That was just one more loss attributable to my idea for the festival. At least we were selling lots of things legitimately. I decided my presence walking among the customers might have a more detrimental effect on the shoplifters than spying down on them from above, so I started walking through the store, keeping my eye out for anyone trying to rip us off.

A little while later, I heard an incessant tapping that I

couldn't place. It sounded as if a lovesick woodpecker was declaring its passion on one of our windowpanes, and it took me longer than it should have to realize that it was the contessa trying to get my attention from above.

I trotted up the stairs and found her standing behind my desk with a scowl plastered on her face. "It took you long enough to get here."

"Things are a little busy on the floor right now," I said.

"Where is Sharon?" she snarled at me as I started to ask her what was so urgent.

"I don't have a clue," I said. "She's your employee, not mine." I was a little more abrupt than I probably should have been, but the woman was already getting on my nerves. If I were Sharon, I'd hide if I could, too.

"If she doesn't get here in time to introduce me, you'll have to do it yourself." She looked like she was as excited by the prospect as I was, which was not at all.

"I'll get one of my siblings to do it," I said. I wanted to keep an eye on things in the store while the contessa gave her presentation. I was getting paranoid about our visitors.

"You'll do it yourself, Ben," she said as she shoved a piece of paper at me. I glanced at her handwritten scrawl and was nearly knocked over by her use of adjectives describing just how wonderful she was. There was no way on earth I could say what she'd written with a straight face.

"Are you sure you wouldn't rather have someone else do this?" I asked.

"I'm positive." She glanced at the clock on my wall. "If Sharon is still not here in two minutes, you'll have to do the honors yourself. I pride myself on punctuality, and I won't let that child thwart me. Two minutes, do you understand me?"

"I get it," I said.

I started to leave in search of Sharon when the contessa asked, "And just where do you think you're going?"

"I thought I'd look for your assistant," I said.

"There's no time for that. You will wait here with me, and we will walk down the stairs together."

"Fine," I said. I watched as the second hand of my clock plodded slowly around twice, hoping for a reprieve, but none came. It appeared that I'd be doing the introductions myself after all.

She offered me her gloved hand, then said, "Shall we?"

"Certainly," I said. Maybe if I fell going down the stairs and broke my leg I wouldn't have to give the introduction. Try as I might, I managed to get down the steps without breaking anything, much to my dismay. She touched my arm at the door in back and said, "When you say my name, project it loudly enough for me to hear you, and I'll enter."

"I'll do my best." As I walked to the microphone, I was frantically searching the gathered crowd, hoping that Sharon was waiting for us out on the sales floor. She was nowhere to be seen. All of the chairs in front of the worktable and microphone were full, and there was standing room only behind them. We'd had to move out some of our shelves in order to accommodate our visitors, and I'd worried about the lost revenue, but at least we were packing people in, and if the number of shopping bags they carried was any indication, the day might just be profitable after all.

I tapped the microphone with my finger and a squeal cut across a dozen conversations like a fan through smoke. "Excuse me," I said a little louder than necessary, causing some of the people sitting near the speakers to wince. "We're ready to get started."

I took a deep breath, then adjusted my voice to the correct volume. "Ladies and gentlemen, it is my privilege and honor to introduce a soapmaking master to you this afternoon." Did she honestly expect me to read it all? There was more of it than I could stomach, so I scanned down a few paragraphs, then flipped the paper over. If the contessa had a problem with my truncated introduction, she was just going to have to deal with it.

Ad-libbing, I said, "Please join me in welcoming our honored guest, the Contessa New Berne."

The applause was heartfelt, but there was no sign of the woman herself. I'd been expecting a grand entrance, but it looked like she wasn't interested in coming out with less than her usual introduction.

As the applause started to die, I tried one more time. "The Contessa New Berne."

It came back up again, but slowed rather quickly, and we were still without our speaker.

I leaned into the microphone and said, "Sorry about that. I'll be right back."

There were a few giggles from the crowd, but many more grumbles. She'd made me look like a fool, and I was prepared to give her a withering remark as I walked to the back room to look for her.

That's when I nearly tripped over the body.

TWO

· · ·

I yelled for help as I leaned over the contessa's still form and searched for a pulse, but I couldn't find one. She was sprawled out on the floor, her carefully pressed clothes askew. I was appalled when I saw there was a bar of soap jammed in her mouth, the custom blend we'd made just for the Soap Celebration. Had she actually choked to death on it? I wanted to pull it out of her mouth, but I had a deadening suspicion that our guest was past helping, and I knew better than to interfere with a crime scene. Molly had lectured me over and over again how everything was important, no matter how insignificant it appeared. Had she tried to fight her killer, or had the murderer struck too quickly for self-defense?

I don't know how anyone heard my plea for help in the boutique, but my brother Jim came crashing through the door three seconds after I shouted out. He's a big guy— husky and solid—and not much gets to him, but when he saw the contessa's body, I saw his knees start to buckle.

"What happened?" Jim stammered as he stared down at her, leaning against the door frame.

"See if there's a doctor out there, then call 911."

He just stood there, staring at her, until I shouted, "Move!"

That got his attention. Jim hurried back to the boutique, and I tried to figure out if there was anything I could do but stand there and guard the body. It was the least I owed her, since the only reason the Contessa New Berne had even been in Harper's Landing was because of me.

Jim came back thirty seconds later with a middle-aged woman right behind him. She brushed past us both when she spotted the contessa lying on the floor. As she checked for any sign of life, I stood back with Jim.

He said softly, "Bob and Jeff are right outside the door. So far we've managed to keep everyone else from knowing what happened. I wouldn't have heard your shout myself if I hadn't been standing near the door."

"Good," I said, and my gaze automatically went to the back door of our business. For the first time since I'd discovered the body, I saw that it was unlatched and partially open.

When I pointed it out to Jim, he said, "You know we keep that door closed and locked all the time. I don't get it."

"Think about it. Either the killer came in that way, or that's how he left," I said. "Molly will have to figure out what happened."

I was sure that door had been closed and locked when I'd escorted the contessa down the stairs. Or was I? Had I really paid that much attention to something I saw every day? As I tried to replay the descent in my mind, I finally decided I couldn't be sure either way.

Jim coughed once, then said, "Listen, I'm sorry I froze up on you like that."

"It's not a problem," I said.

"It just shocked me, seeing her like that."

I put a hand on my brother's shoulder. "There's nothing to apologize for. You did fine."

He shrugged. "I'd appreciate it if you didn't mention it to anyone else."

"Mention what?" I asked him, offering a slight smile.

"Thanks." Jim had a reputation, both among the family and the community, that he was tough—blunt and abrupt—and if the conception was that important to him, I didn't mind. Me, I didn't care if the whole world knew that stumbling across a dead body had a way of shaking me to my core.

"I can't help her," the doctor finally said. "I'm afraid what you need is a coroner."

"This had to have just happened," I said. "I was with her five minutes ago."

She shrugged. "If I had to guess, I'd say she died pretty quickly."

"Did the soap choke her to death?" Jim asked.

Cleaning her hands with a shop towel, the doctor stood as she said, "No, I found a head wound in back that appeared to go pretty deep. My guess is that someone hit her from behind with the claw end of a hammer or something like that."

I could see where the blood was starting to star out its stain near the contessa's head. "So why was the soap shoved halfway down her throat?" I asked.

"If I were to guess, I'd have to say there's some significance to it that we don't know yet. I'm afraid that's all I can tell you right now."

"Thank you," I said as I offered her my hand without thinking. "I'm Ben Perkins, and this is my brother Jim."

She started to shake my hand, but then must have realized that despite her cleaning attempts, she was in no position to return the courtesy. "I'm Karen Weiss. I'm a dermatologist, and I've got to tell you, I haven't seen a blunt force trauma since my turn at an emergency room in Virginia."

"I'm just glad you were here," I said.

"I didn't do anything, honestly. I'm from Hickory, and I drove up when I heard you were hosting the contessa. I'm a huge fan." She glanced down at the body, then corrected herself. "I was, I should say. I'm really sorry I couldn't help her."

Molly rushed in, dressed in her police uniform, with my brother Jeff on her heels. They'd been dating for a few months, and they were getting pretty serious. I'd had a tough time with their relationship at first—since I'd dated Molly through high school and some time beyond it—but I was finally at the point where I was happy for them both. It was hard enough finding love in this world, and if they had discovered it in each other, I was determined to be happy for them.

"Has anybody touched anything?" Molly asked. Now why was she looking so hard at me when she asked that?

Doctor Weiss answered for me. "I didn't disturb anything, but I did check the victim for a pulse. She was dead when I got here."

"From the soap?" Molly asked.

"No, it was a blunt force trauma. I can show you if you'd like."

"That would be great," Molly said. "But give me one second first." She whispered something into her radio, then she moved toward the body, with Jeff close behind.

Molly turned to him and said, "You need to help Bob guard the door."

I'd expected him to put up some kind of resistance, but he just nodded and left us. It was amazing to see the changes that love had wrought in both of them. There had been a softness in her voice when she'd ordered him to return to his station, and that had startled me nearly as much as finding the contessa's body.

After thirty seconds of the doctor's explanation, Molly stood up. "Thanks, Doc. Could you stick around for a while?"

"I'd be happy to, though I'm not sure what good I can do."

"I just need to get a statement from you."

Molly turned to me then and said, "Ben, you might as well know that I've sealed off the front exit so I can interview everyone here. We're keeping it as low-key as we can right now, but when your customers find out what happened here, they're not going to be happy about being forced to stay."

So that's what she had whispered into her radio earlier. "Molly, nobody in there had anything to do with this. The back door was open when I found her. I've got a hundred customers in there right now."

She looked at me steadily. "I hate to interfere with your business, but I've got a murder to solve. No one leaves until one of my officers talks to them, understood?"

"Yeah, I know you're right. But Mom's going to want to talk to you about it." I knew Molly wasn't anymore interested in getting chewed out by my mother than any of the rest of us, but there wasn't much chance she was going to avoid a scolding, and she knew it. Molly frowned at me, then started talking to her office on her radio, dismissing me and the doctor from her thoughts completely.

Doctor Weiss frowned, so I asked her, "Is there something wrong?"

"I was hoping to get some shopping done," she admitted.

"Molly," I said as she put her radio back on its belt clip. "Would it be all right if the doctor browses in the shop while she waits for you? She'll be right there if you need her."

"What? That's fine. Just so she doesn't wander off."

The doctor squeezed my arm. "Thank you so much."

"Tell you what. Come find me when you're ready to check out. I'll give you a discount." My mother wouldn't like it, I knew that without even asking, but the way I looked at it, the doctor had done us a service, and I hated for the books not to balance.

"I appreciate the thought, but my hobbies are my only vices, so I can afford to indulge them."

"Why don't you go with her?" Molly asked. "And take your brothers with you."

"I thought you needed them for sentry duty."

"Thanks, but some of my people will be here any minute. Tell Jeff for me, would you?"

I nodded. "I'll take care of it. Is there any way we could get the ambulance driver to come in through the back door?"

"I've already taken care of it," she said. "They have their instructions to come in that way."

"Thanks," I said, then almost as an afterthought, I added, "It wouldn't hurt to check that back door for prints."

The scorn in her gaze was readily obvious. "Thanks for the crimebuster tip, but I actually thought of that myself."

"Hey, I'm just trying to help," I said.

"I understand," she replied, her voice more gentle. "Ben, you know how homicides on my turf make me cranky."

I nodded, then decided to take her advice and go back out front before I managed to get myself in any trouble. I'd been the last person to see the contessa alive; besides the killer, at any rate. While I hadn't been all that fond of Contessa New Berne during our brief acquaintance, I'd had no reason to want her dead. Even without the homicide, the red ink we were experiencing would assure that this would be the first and last Soap Celebration we ever had at our shop.

I found Jeff and Jim guarding the door between the boutique and the factory sections of our business.

"You guys can go," I said. "Molly's got reinforcements on the way."

"I'll stay," Jeff said. "Someone could still try to get through."

He looked at me as if he were daring me to demand he leave his post, but in all honesty, I didn't care.

"Suit yourself," I said as I brushed past him. I wanted to find Diana to tell her what had happened, but she wasn't near the book table, and I couldn't find her anywhere else in the shop. People were still in their seats, and I realized that they didn't know the contessa was dead. I'd forgotten all about the planned presentation the second I'd stumbled over the body.

I made my way to the microphone, trying furiously to think of something to say to them. Finally, I announced, "I'm sorry to say that today's talk and demonstration have been canceled."

There were some angry murmurs coming from the crowd, and a lot of them were directed at me.

"Why won't she do it?" a woman in front asked. "I saw her. She was just here."

A man with a crusty frown asked, "Where is she? Did she walk out on us?"

Another voice said, "You're both wrong. I don't think she even bothered to show up."

I held up my hands, waiting for them to stop while I tried to come up with something to tell them. There was no easy way to put it. "The contessa is dead," I said. That shut them up, so I added quickly, "And the police want to interview each of you before you leave."

That caused the uproar I'd been expecting all along. Making a half-hearted attempt at salvaging something from the mess, I added, "Why not take the time to shop while you wait? We're offering a 20 percent discount on everything in the store as a way of apologizing for any inconvenience this might cause you."

At least that quieted them down. Mom rushed up to me less than two seconds after I'd finished my announcement. "Benjamin Perkins, have you lost your mind? Do you have any idea how much you just cost us?"

Normally I would take the chiding and move on, but I wasn't in the mood. "Tell me something, Mom, how much would we lose if we didn't offer them anything? Having a homicide on the premises isn't going to put our customers in a buying mood. Besides, I was kind of hoping it would distract them from realizing what just happened." I paused a second, then added, "I'm fine, by the way, though I nearly tumbled over the body when I found her lying there on the floor." I didn't mention the bar of soap shoved halfway down her throat. Mom would learn about that soon enough—hopefully from someone else.

"Benjamin, I'm sorry," Mom said, her tone contrite. "You did the right thing."

"Thanks," I said. "Now if you'll excuse me, I need to find Diana."

Mom looked puzzled. "She left right after you went in back to get the contessa. I must say, Diana's face was the ghastliest shade of white, and when I tried to ask her what was wrong, she acted as though she didn't even hear me. Did you two have a fight, Ben?"

"Not that I know of," I admitted, though I'd had altercations in the past with girlfriends without really having a clue what I'd said or done to make them mad.

"I'm sure it's nothing," Mom said. "Still, you should find her and talk to her."

"That's a good idea," I said as I headed for the front door. The only problem was that I couldn't get out. A beefy young cop who looked like he gobbled steroids was standing just outside the door, and I doubted I could force my way through with all three brothers' help. Diana must not have had any trouble leaving, though. She'd gone before I'd discovered the body. But why had she left without saying anything to me? She could have at least mentioned her abrupt departure to one of my siblings. I'd have to check with them all just in case she had, but in the meantime, several of our customers were taking advantage of my discount offer and were loading up their baskets with scents, soaps, and kits. Even with the price break, we'd still at least make something. It might have been cold-hearted to think that way, but there was nothing I could do to help Contessa New Berne, and my family needed to make a living. We had an awful lot of mouths to feed.

There was a disturbance at the front door, and I turned

to see what the yelling was about. I recognized Sharon, Contessa New Berne's assistant, immediately. She was struggling to get past the cop at the door.

I tried to push past him, and the oaf snapped at me, "You're not allowed out. Get back inside."

"Ben, tell him I belong in there. I overslept, and the contessa's going to kill me for being late."

"It's all right," I told the cop, "She's the victim's assistant," I added, without realizing what I was blurting out.

Sharon crumbled. "Did something happen to Connie? She can't be dead. Is this some kind of sick joke?"

"I'm sorry. She was murdered," I admitted.

With a wail of despair, Sharon collapsed against me, sobbing in hysteria.

"I'm bringing her inside," I said, doing my best to console her.

"No one comes in or goes out," he protested. "Those are my orders."

"I don't care what your orders are. She needs my help," I said.

"It could be a trick," he answered.

"Get out of our way," I demanded, and he finally stepped aside as I led her into the shop. Sharon didn't look that heavy, but she was dead weight against me as I staggered to the break room to put her on our couch. There were a few murmurs from the crowd, but for the most part they moved aside as I neared them. Bless my sister Louisa. She'd seen where I was heading and met me at the door to the break room.

"Bring her in here," she said as she opened the door and stepped out of my way. "What happened?"

"She fell apart when I told her the contessa was dead," I admitted as I helped her to the couch.

Louisa got a washcloth, doused it with cold water, then
applied it to Sharon's forehead.

Her hard, gasping sobs finally started to ease.

"Are you all right?" I asked gently.

"No, but I will be," she said as she pressed the cloth to
her head. "I'm feeling a little better now. I'm sorry I made
such a scene."

"You had every right to act the way you did."

"The shock of it hit me like a club. I can't believe she's
gone."

"You called her Connie before you passed out. Was that
her real name?"

Sharon nodded, holding the washcloth in place with
one hand as she straightened up. "It was such a secret to
the world, you know? I even had to sign a nondisclosure
agreement that I wouldn't tell anyone her real name,
ever."

"I guess you're free of that now, aren't you?"

Sharon shook her head. "You'd think so, but no. It was
worded most carefully. As long as I'm alive, I'm not allowed
to say her name aloud. I'd appreciate it if you wouldn't tell
anyone what I said."

Before I could reply, Louisa said, "Don't worry, child,
we didn't hear a thing."

"Thanks," she said. "How about you, Ben?"

"I won't say anything, but you can bet that cop out front
will mention it to his boss."

Sharon shrugged. "The contessa used to tell me not to
worry about anything I couldn't control. I'm going to miss
her."

"What happens to you now?" I asked.

I'd meant it to be a thoughtful question, so I was surprised by her reaction. With a tremor in her voice, she said,

"I don't know. This job was all I had." And then she started sobbing again.

"What? What did I say?" I looked over at Louisa to see if I'd said anything inadvertently, but she shook her head, evidently as confused by the outburst as I'd been.

"I'm sorry," Sharon said after a moment's pause. "I'm just going to be so lost without her."

I leaned down toward her and asked, "Would you like me to get a doctor? We've got one in the boutique shopping right now." I was going to make sure Doctor Weiss received an extra 30 percent off, as well as getting the 20 we were giving everyone else.

"No, I'll be fine. I just need a few seconds to accept this."

Louisa and I were trying to decide what to do when Molly walked in, a scowl on her face.

"Are you the assistant?" she asked Sharon.

"I am. This is just awful."

Molly said, "If you two will excuse us, we need to talk."

I wasn't about to let her just kick us out without a fight. "Should the ladies step outside, or should you and I go somewhere else where we can have some privacy?"

"Funny, Ben. Go on. You and Louisa take off."

My sister and I stepped outside so Molly could interview Sharon. I tried to listen in at the door, but Louisa said, "Give it up. I've been trying for years, and I've never heard a word I could understand."

"You've been spying on your brothers and sisters?" I asked, trying my best to feign shock.

"Not just them, I've tried it with Mom and Grandpa, too. They built this place too well, if you ask me."

"I guess," I said as I scanned the crowd of shoppers. I don't know how long we waited outside the break room, but the door finally reopened and Molly came out, with Sharon on her heels.

"Remember what I said," Molly said to her as she moved toward the front door.

"What did she say?" Louisa asked before I could.

"I can't leave town," Sharon admitted. "She thinks I might be able to help her solve the contessa's murder. I wasn't even here. How can I be of any help to her?"

"You might know more than you realize," I said.

Sharon sounded desolate as she asked, "Why did this have to happen here, of all places?"

I jumped all over that statement. "What's so bad about Harper's Landing?"

Sharon looked startled as she replied, "Forget you heard that. I should learn to keep my mouth shut."

"Well, it's a little too late for that," Louisa said. "We heard you call her Connie, so you might as well tell us the rest of it."

"You weren't even nearby when I said that," Sharon said shrilly.

"I was right behind Ben. You must not have seen me," Louisa said.

I thought my sister was lying, too, but I couldn't be sure.

Sharon looked as though she wanted to cry, and I said softly, "We'll keep both of your secrets, as long as you told the police the truth."

"That's the only reason I'm telling you now," Sharon said. "That policewoman Molly made me tell her, and I know it won't be long before the whole town knows. The contessa's real name was Connie Brown. She's been in Harper's Landing before."

The name was familiar, but I couldn't quite remember why. "Now where have I heard that name?"

Sharon looked miserable as she admitted, "It was a long time ago, but she was driving drunk and killed a couple coming home from a party; she got off with not much more than a slap on the wrist."

And suddenly I knew where I'd heard the name before. Connie Brown had killed Diana's parents a long time ago, and I had to wonder if my girlfriend had gotten her revenge in my family's soap shop.

THREE

○ ○ ○

I really needed to talk to Diana now. "Excuse me," I said as I ducked into the break room so I could call the bookstore. Rufus—Diana's clerk and coworker at Dying To Read—hadn't seen his boss all day, and she wasn't answering her cellular phone. I thought about trying her aunt and uncle's house, but I couldn't remember their last name for the life of me, though we'd met a couple of times in the past.

Molly was interviewing customers at the front door as they left when I walked back out onto the sales floor, and at least some of them were carrying bags from our shop. The contessa, or more rightfully, Connie Brown—which was how I was going to start referring to her in my mind, because the title was a little much, honestly—had met an unhappy end in our shop, and I felt terrible that I'd been the cause of her demise, no matter how indirectly. Still, there was no sense wishing ill for the store. I was surprised by how quickly Molly was clearing the customers out, so

I moved up front to hear just what she was asking each of them. It didn't take long before she had a new person in front of her.

Molly asked, in rapid-fire order, "Did you see Contessa New Berne alive today or yesterday? Did you know Connie Brown, or what she did? Do you know anything that might help our investigation into the murder?"

When she got null responses to all of her questions, she said, "Give your name and address to Officer Higgins. He'll need to see a photo ID as well. Next," she called out.

I slipped past the next woman in line. Molly started asking her questions before she realized it was me. "I need to get outside," I said, interrupting her.

"You need to stay right where you are," Molly said. "You, more than anyone else here. When I'm through with your customers, we'll have time to talk."

"I need to find Diana," I said.

"Don't you think that's my priority at the moment, too? I've got half our police force out looking for her."

Why was I not surprised? "Molly, you can't honestly think that Diana had anything to do with the murder."

"You bet your soap on a rope I do," she said. "She had more reason than anyone else in town to want to harm that woman. I need to find her."

"I'm not denying that she had a motive," I said as calmly as I could muster. "But there have to be other suspects in your mind. What about Sharon?"

"Her assistant?" Molly asked. "What does she have to gain from killing her boss? All she gets out of it is the hassle of looking for another job."

"How do you know that's true? For all we know, Sharon could be her sole heir."

"What have you heard, Ben?" There was a sharpness to her question, like a shark going after bleeding prey.

"I haven't heard anything," I admitted, "but that doesn't mean it couldn't be true. It's all conjecture at this point," I said. "I just don't want you focusing on Diana and letting the real murderer get away."

Molly shook her head. "And none of this has anything to do with the fact that my prime suspect just happens to be your girlfriend, does it?"

"Of course it does," I said a little louder than I'd intended to. "But just because I'm prejudiced doesn't mean she's not innocent."

Molly shook her head in disgust. "Ben, go back inside. I don't have time for this right now."

I was about to protest when I saw Diana coming up the steps. I tried to motion her away, but she must have thought I was waving at her, because she hurried up to Molly and me.

"Hi, Ben. What's going on? Sorry I had to duck out, but I spilled a drink on my outfit so I had to go home and change. Hi, Molly. What's wrong?"

Molly pulled her aside as she said, "I've got the entire force out looking for you. You're in some real trouble, Diana."

"What did I do?" she asked with total innocence. "Is it about that stop sign? Listen, I'm sorry I didn't come to a complete stop, but no one else was around. I was in a hurry to get back here, I knew the contessa had probably already started her presentation, and I had to be back here before she finished. I'm really sorry."

"The contessa is dead," I said, and Molly gave me a dirty look.

Diana looked honestly surprised by the news. "Oh, no. What happened to her?"

Before I could answer, Molly put a hand roughly over my mouth. "Let me handle this."

"Ben? What's going on?" There was a hint of panic in her voice, and I could see that she was worried. I couldn't blame her. She might not have known it yet, but she had every right to be.

I pulled my mouth away from Molly's hand and said, "The contessa's real name was Connie Brown."

Diana reacted exactly as if I'd just shot her. Without a word, a whimper, or a sigh, she collapsed on the porch in front of Where There's Soap as if she were a puppet and someone had just cut her strings.

"Nice, Ben, really nice," Molly said as she knelt down to check Diana's pulse. After a few moments, she added, "Well, she's not dead, you can be thankful for that, at least. Help me get her inside, could you?"

I was helping far too many distraught women into our break room lately. We managed to get Diana inside, and another officer took over Molly's routine questioning out front. There was no doubt Diana was her sole suspect at the moment.

"Shouldn't we do something?" I asked Molly as I looked at Diana.

"I sent Nate Green to get the smelling salts from my first aid kit. He'll be right back."

"I don't want to wait. Let me see if Dr. Weiss is still here."

Molly shook her head. "Sorry, I let her go ten minutes ago. Ben, don't worry, she's going to be fine."

Though I was feeling useless, there was one thing I could do while we waited for the smelling salts. It was time to call in some help, only I didn't want to have to dial the number I knew I had to call.

KELLY Sheer picked up on the third ring. She was a former girlfriend of mine, but more importantly, Kelly was the best criminal lawyer in our part of North Carolina. No matter what might have happened between us in the past, she was the only person I'd even consider calling when someone I cared about was in trouble.

"Hi, Kelly. It's Ben," I said.

"Ben, how nice to hear your voice," Kelly said cordially. The last time we'd spoken, she'd been in tears, so it was nice to hear some pleasure in her voice.

I wasn't sure how long it would last, though. "I need your help."

Molly's eyebrows went up as she heard me say that, but I didn't care what she thought about me at that moment.

"Anything. Just name it." Kelly was being much too agreeable, but I had a suspicion that was about to end.

"A woman was murdered at the soap boutique today. It turns out that a long time ago, she killed Diana Long's parents when she was driving drunk. Nobody knew who she was when she came here for a presentation today, but Molly is convinced that Diana killed her."

"I didn't say that," Molly snapped, but I ignored her.

"Where is she right now?" Kelly asked, the light and easy tone gone from her voice. She was all business now, in her full shark-attack mode that had scared just about every prosecutor she'd ever faced.

"As soon as Diana wakes up from her fainting spell, Molly is going to question her about the murder, and I'd like you here as soon as you can get here."

Molly wanted to say something else—it was apparent in her stance and the grim lines of her lips—but she kept quiet.

"I don't know," Kelly said at last. "I'm not sure I could do a proper job helping her."

"Listen, don't you think I know how awkward this is for both of us? I wouldn't have asked you if it wasn't important. Kelly, you said you'd do anything, and this is the only thing I want."

There was another long pause, then she sighed. "When she wakes up, tell her not to say anything until I get there. I'm coming right over. And Ben, don't leave her side until you've delivered my message. I don't care if the building's on fire, do you understand?"

"I promise. And Kelly?"

"What?"

"Thanks," I said.

After I hung up, Molly said, "You just had to butt in, didn't you?"

"Diana has a right to legal representation," I said. "She's in no position to do anything about it herself, so I'm doing it for her."

"I can't believe you had the guts to call your old girlfriend to represent your new one. I've been out with you myself, Ben. Trust me when I say I'm not trying to offend you, but I don't get it. Why would she agree to help either one of you?"

"I don't know, and I'm not going to ask," I said. "I just want the best for Diana, and Kelly is the best we've got."

"I can't wait to see Diana's face when Kelly walks through the door."

At the sound of her name, Diana groaned a few times, then opened her eyes. We hadn't even needed the smelling salts to revive her. She'd only been out about a minute, but it had seemed like an eternity to me as she lay there, helpless. Diana sat up on the couch, then looked at Molly and me with confusion. "What's going on? What happened?" A frown suddenly creased her mouth. "Oh, no, I remember now. It really happened, didn't it?"

Before Molly could say anything, I said, "Kelly Sheer's on her way here to represent you. She said not to say anything to Molly until she arrives."

Diana looked at me as if I'd lost my mind. "Who called her? Ben, did you honestly think I'd let her represent me in anything? The woman hates me, and I'm not so sure I don't return the feeling in full. She'd probably let me hang for this purely out of spite."

I knelt down beside the couch, trying to ignore the smirk on Molly's face. She was enjoying this way too much. "Listen," I said as calmly as I could, "you need to have her here looking out for your interests. She's the very best attorney I know, and no matter what you two think of each other, we need her. Do you understand me?"

Diana didn't like it anymore than Kelly had; I didn't need to be a mind reader to know that. But after a few seconds, she finally nodded her agreement. "I'll behave myself if she does."

"That's all I can ask," I said. That wasn't anywhere near the truth, but I'd take it, at least for the moment.

The three of us stayed in the break room until there was a knock at the door three minutes after I'd hung up with Kelly. She must have run a stop sign or two herself to get here that fast.

"Have you said anything to anyone?" she asked Diana.

"No," she answered briefly.

"Good. Let's keep it that way." She looked hard at

Diana as she asked, "Do you have any problem with me representing you in this matter?"

"I suppose not," Diana said curtly.

"Good." Ignoring me completely, Kelly turned to Molly and said, "I want my client examined by a physician before you question her further. I'm concerned she may be suffering from some type of physical trauma."

Molly said, "I don't know about her, but I have a woman in the other room with her head bashed in. All I'm trying to do is figure out who did it."

Molly was embellishing the truth a little, but she did have a point. If it had been someone I didn't know under her intense scrutiny, I would have been the first person to cheer her on. I didn't want a murderer running loose in Harper's Landing any more than the rest of the community did. But I wouldn't believe Diana capable of it, no matter what the impetus. Still, Molly had once told me that anybody, and she meant absolutely anybody, could be a killer, given the right circumstances. I wasn't sure I believed her, but she'd made her point then, and her words drifted back to haunt me now.

Kelly must have sympathized with Molly's directive, too, if only a little bit. "Let me get her examined, and then we'll come by your office for an interview. Is that fair enough?"

"No, but I don't have much choice, do I? Just don't take too long, counselor. Don't make me come looking for you."

"I wouldn't dream of it," Kelly said.

Molly stared at me a second longer than she had to, then she walked out of the break room. It appeared that it took every ounce of her restraint not to slam the door behind her.

"Thanks for coming on such short notice," I said to Kelly.

She gave me much the same look Molly had, and I was

getting tired of being treated like I was the one who was guilty. "We need some time to talk, Ben."

"I don't see how we could manage that right now," I said. "There's a lot going on here."

"I don't mean you, I'm talking about Diana."

This dismissal was clear enough. I was being invited to leave my family's break room entirely more than I liked, but I knew I had to go.

Before I left, though, I asked Diana, "Is that all right with you?"

She nodded, so I took off. One of a man's worst nightmares is to have his ex-girlfriend in the same room with his current one, and I was not only living it, I'd been the one to set it up. I just hoped they were too busy talking about Connie Brown to compare notes on me.

After ten minutes—time I spent hovering nearby— Kelly and Diana came out of the break room together.

"That was quick," I said.

"We're not finished. We're just moving our conversation to the hospital."

Diana protested, "I keep telling you, I'm fine. All I got was a knot on my head when I fell. It's nothing."

Kelly whispered, "We don't know that until you're examined by an accredited physician, now do we? So, are we going to the hospital, or do you want to head straight to police headquarters?"

Diana didn't even need to think about it. "Let's go get a checkup." As she started to leave, she called out to me, "I'll call you later, Ben."

Kelly didn't miss a beat as she added, "And you'd better believe I will, too."

After they were gone, my mother came over to me. "Is it finally over?"

Our customers were all gone, and as I'd feared, none of them had come back in after the police had questioned them. I shrugged. "Our part of it is for now," I said. "Mom, I'm sorry about all this."

"None of it was your fault," she said gently. "Who knew our guest of honor would be murdered in the back hallway?" Mom shivered, then added, "Jim told me the ambulance left ten minutes ago."

"How about the production line? Can the guys get started on their next run?" Getting our family back in the business of soapmaking was the best thing that could happen for all of us right now. Sometimes I complained that things were too quiet in our business, but right now, I would have given anything to have this day be boring.

Mom shook her head. "No, the police said we won't be able to use it until tomorrow. That includes our offices, too, Ben. We might as well shut the store down and go home. We're finished, at least for today."

I glanced at my watch and saw that we had two hours left in our working day. It was a first for Mom if she was willing to lock up early.

"You all can go ahead," I said, "but I'm staying. At least I can clean up." We'd rearranged the entire sales floor to fit in the contessa's talk and book signing, and seeing the disarray when we came back the next day would only bring back all of the events we'd be trying desperately to forget.

A bright spark came into her eyes. "That's a wonderful idea. The sooner we can get the store back to normal, the better off we'll all be." She clapped her hands, a sure sign that she wanted a family meeting. My brothers and sisters gathered around, and Mom said, "Ben's had a wonderful idea. Instead of going home early and taking the rest of the day off, we're all going to stay here and clean up."

"Wee," Jim said.

"Just what I wanted to do with my spare time," Kate added.

Jeff shrugged. "Why not? We need to do it sooner or later."

Louisa groaned. "I choose later."

"Enough," Mom said. "We run this business as a family, and we'll take this blow as a family. Now let's get busy."

Everybody found something to do, and I appointed myself the job of packing all the soapmaking books we'd brought in for the signing back in their boxes. Bob came over and said, "You need any help?"

"That would be great," I said. "These won't fit in my Miata. After we get them loaded up, we can take them back to Diana's bookstore. You sure you don't mind giving me a hand?"

"Compared to some of the other jobs around here, that's the best offer I've had."

After the boxes were tucked safely in their cartons, Jim and Jeff helped us load them into the back of Bob's truck without even being asked. Once we had them all in place, Bob said, "Let's go, Ben. Hop in."

As we drove to the bookstore, he added, "I can't believe somebody was murdered in our shop today. It's kind of tough to accept, isn't it?"

"I'm having a hard time with it, too," I admitted.

"I guess you would," Bob said.

"What do you mean by that?"

"Easy, big brother. I just mean that having your girl-friend accused of murder can't be an easy thing to take."

"It's not," I admitted. After a few seconds, I added, "Sorry if I jumped on you, Bob. I guess I am a little stressed."

"You've got every right to be. Was it bad, finding the body like that?"

I bit my lip, then said, "To be honest with you, it's something I'd rather forget about right now."

My brother nodded as he drove on in silence. A few minutes later I heard him laughing softly to himself.

"What's so funny?"

"Sorry, Ben. It's nothing."

"No, share it with me, please. If there's something funny about this situation, I'd love to hear it."

Bob hesitated, then finally he said, "Man, I couldn't believe it when Kelly walked through the door. Then when I heard you were the one who called her, I thought you must have lost your mind. You've got guts, I'll give you that."

"I just wish it made up for brains," I said. "They both want to talk to me later, and I've got a feeling I'm not going to enjoy either conversation."

Bob smiled smugly. "I love being married. That way I just have to worry about one woman being mad at me. You're going to have a ton of them upset with you, at the rate you're going."

"I did what I had to do," I said as we pulled up in front of the bookstore.

I told Bob, "Wait here a second, would you? I need to talk to Rufus before we start carrying books in."

The clerk was sitting behind the register reading something dark, and when I spoke his name, the college kid nearly fell off his stool. "Don't sneak up on me like that, Ben."

"Sorry, I didn't realize that I had. What are you reading?"

He pushed the book aside. "I've seen your taste in books. Trust me, you wouldn't like it."

"You're a powerful salesman, aren't you?"

He shrugged. "I know my books, and I know my customers. It's a real bummer about Diana, isn't it? Have they arrested her yet?" He seemed a little too eager to have his speculation confirmed.

"She's getting a checkup at the hospital right now," I said. "When she heard about the murder, she fainted and hit her head."

"Man. Is she going to be okay?"

"I think so, but we all thought that it would be a good idea to make sure." I asked him, "Hey, how did you hear about it so quickly? I know Harper's Landing is small, but this just happened."

"One of your customers at Where There's Soap happens to shop here, too. She came straight to the bookstore as soon as she heard about what happened. What I don't get is why they think Diana had anything to do with it."

So he hadn't heard everything. "The murder victim's real name was Connie Brown."

It was the first time I'd ever seen Rufus speechless. After ten seconds, he said, "It can't be the same woman. It just can't be."

"I'm afraid it was," I said.

"Oh, man, no wonder they want to arrest her. Has she got a good lawyer?"

"I called Kelly Sheer," I admitted. "She agreed to represent her."

Rufus whooped with delight. "You're kidding me, right? Do you have any idea what Diana thinks of her? No, you couldn't have, or you never would have called the lady."

"She needed someone good to represent her," I said.

"Listen, we've got a truckload of books outside that we're not going to need. Where can we put them?"

Rufus thought about it a second, then said, "Why don't you bring them around back? You can stack them near the door until Diana can decide what to do with them. She's got a little more on her mind right now than returns, you know what I mean?" He handed me a key as he said it. "That will unlock the door."

"Aren't you going to meet us back there?" I asked.

"Somebody's got to watch the store," he said as he picked his book back up.

"Thanks, I'll be sure to tell Diana that you were the model employee in her time of need."

"I'd appreciate that," he said, missing my jab entirely. "I've been pushing her for a raise for months, but so far I haven't had any luck."

I shook my head as I walked back outside.

Bob was leaning against the side of the truck as if he were guarding the cargo. "What's up?"

"We need to take these around back," I said as I got inside. Bob joined me, then circled the block and pulled up beside the bookstore's loading dock.

"Sorry we're not getting any help," I said as I unlocked the back door.

He lowered the truck's tailgate, then said, "Are you kidding? Carrying boxes beats sweeping up back at the shop. I never have minded a little physical labor."

After we got the books transferred to the back, I told Bob, "I'll meet you out front. I'm going to give Rufus this key back."

"Suits me. And take your time, Ben. I meant what I said. I'm not in any rush to get to the shop."

I started to walk through the back of the store when

I popped my head into Diana's office. I suppose I was being a little nosy, but I didn't think she'd mind. There was a new photograph on her desk, one that had just been taken a few days before. We were picnicking out in front of the bookstore, and Rufus must have snapped our picture without me realizing it.

I walked up front to return the key, and as I handed it over, I asked, "Have you been stalking me?"

He looked at me carefully before he asked, "What are you talking about?"

"I went into Diana's office and I saw a new picture of us together. Funny thing was, I don't remember posing for it."

Rufus looked uncomfortable for a second, then he asked, "So what were you doing in Diana's office?"

I couldn't admit I'd been snooping, could I? "I had to use the phone."

"Then why didn't I see a line light up?" he asked as he pointed to his bank of telephones.

"I was going to, but then I saw that picture. That kind of creeped me out, if you know what I mean."

When he didn't answer, I pushed him harder. "I want to know what you've been up to, Rufus. If you won't tell me, I'll have the police ask you."

Reluctantly, he admitted, "I just got a zoom lens for my Nikon and I wanted to try it out. You two were over there laughing and having a good time, so I took a picture. I've been taking all kinds of shots. Sorry if it bothers you. Diana was thrilled with it."

That was innocent enough. "Fine. I'm sorry if I overreacted. Just one thing, okay?"

He was expecting a lecture, that much was clear. "What's that?"

"I'd like a copy, too."

That surprised him. "Sure thing. I've got tons of candid shots, if you'd like to look through the negatives." He looked down at his hands, then added, "I even took a bunch of shots today before the store opened, but I won't get around to developing the negatives until later."

I shook my head. "No thanks. Rufus, why don't you stick to birds from now on, okay?"

"Spoilsport," he said, then dismissing me, Rufus went back to his book.

Bob and I drove back to Where There's Soap, and to our displeasure, it appeared that my family had decided to cut the cake Mom had made for the signing without waiting for us.

"We couldn't let it just go to waste," Mom said.

"This is so good," Jeff said, sticking an entire flower made of icing into his mouth.

"Move over, Junior. I want a piece."

Cindy handed me a sliver of cake and said, "I cut one for you already."

I looked at it as if it were tainted. "You call that a slice? Let me have the knife."

Louisa laughed, and I asked her, "What's so funny?"

"I told her you wouldn't go for it," she said. "But she insisted." Louisa patted my belly, which was a little larger than it needed to be, but not by that much. "She thinks you should start cutting back on your calories now that you're getting older."

"I didn't say that at all," Cindy protested. Then she added sheepishly, "At least not that badly."

"You're absolutely right," I said. "I do need to start cutting back."

Louisa's smile died on her face, and then I added, "And

I will, starting tomorrow. Or the next day. Thursday at the latest."

All my siblings started laughing as I cut an extremely generous slice to accompany the puny offering Cindy had given me.

Bob smiled at me and said, "I'll take one just like it."

Kate said, "You know Jessica isn't going to like that."

Bob cut a big piece nonetheless. "What my wife doesn't know won't hurt me." Just before taking the first bite, he added, "You're not going to say anything to her, are you?"

There was a battery of insincere denials, and Bob reluctantly put half his cake onto another plate. "I can't believe my own family is so willing to tell on me," he said.

Jeff laughed as he snagged the extra piece. "I'll take it, if you don't want it."

After we'd all shared some cake and punch, Mom said, "Now let's finish this up. We've got a big day ahead of us tomorrow."

We all worked together cleaning and rearranging the store, and the boutique section of our shop was soon neat and organized again. I gathered the posters we'd had made up of the contessa and started to carry them out through the production line in back toward the Dumpsters that were tucked behind a screen near the employee parking area. When the door wouldn't budge, I remembered the police weren't finished there and that they had locked us out. As I carried the posters outside along the side of the building where our customers normally parked, I was surprised to see someone getting out of her car in one of the patron parking spaces. I thought all of our customers had given up on us for the day.

Then I saw that it wasn't a shopper at all.

FOUR

○ ○ ○

AS soon as I saw her face, I could tell that Sharon had been crying; the last thing I wanted to do was intrude on her private grief. I tried going back the way I'd come, but she spotted me, and there was no way I could just ignore her.

"Ben, do you have a second?" she asked as she dabbed at her cheeks.

"Sure," I said. Crying women had always made me uncomfortable. I never knew what to do, but I hated to just stand there, helpless.

After Sharon approached me, she said, "I'm sorry. I just don't know where else to go."

"Would you like to come inside the shop?"

"Would we be alone in there?" she asked.

"No, but it's just my family. Maybe we could help." If I got her within shouting distance of my mother and sisters, I wouldn't have to worry about consoling Sharon myself. The female members of my family were adept at dealing with emotion, while my brothers and I, with varying degrees of ineptitude, were not.

"Honestly, I'm not sure I could ever go back inside there," she said.

I could understand that reaction. "Would you like to sit in the garden and talk instead? There's a bench that's perfect for private conversations."

My family, like most folks who made custom soaps, had its own flower and herb garden. Not only was it a great deal less expensive growing some of our own supplies than buying them, but we were always sure of the quality. My father, a born romantic if ever there was one, had insisted that the garden be laid out with a bench in its center, and he and my mother had spent many pleasant evenings there together, holding hands and laughing on into the night. I missed my dad, but nobody missed him more than my mother did.

She frowned as she stared at the bench. "It's a little public, don't you think? We could go for a walk instead, if you don't mind. It might be easier to talk that way."

"That's fine with me," I said. As I led her down the block past a shuttered jewelry store, I asked, "I never had the chance to ask. Were you and Connie close?"

"I guess I can drop the act of calling her the contessa, can't I? It won't be long before the whole world knows. I worked with her for three years," Sharon admitted. "I still can't believe she's gone." Sharon stopped abruptly and turned into my arms. "Ben, what am I going to do?"

As she started sobbing again, I did my best to comfort her. Finally, the wracking tears subsided.

"I'm so sorry," she said. "Sometimes I'm such a girl. That's two crying jags in one day. Normally I can go months without shedding a single tear."

"You're allowed," I said. "You've had a rough day."

We started walking again, and she dabbed at her cheeks as she said, "Breaking down right now isn't going to do anyone any good, is it?" She sniffed a few times, then said, "There. I'm better now."

"Are you sure you feel like talking? I understand if you'd rather not. It's a nice day. We could just walk around town and try to forget about what happened today."

"No, I need to say this out loud so I can accept it. I've been trying to think about who had reason to want Connie dead, and unfortunately, there's a bigger list than I wanted to admit at first."

Our conversation was suddenly getting very interesting. "Did you say anything about your suspects to Molly?"

"Who's Molly again?"

"The police officer you talked to earlier," I explained. I wanted to hear what Sharon had to say, but I knew how Molly would react if I didn't suggest the assistant speak with her first.

"Oh, yes, I know who she is. I plan to talk to her the next time I see her," Sharon said, "but I wanted to get my thoughts in order before I did. She's intimidating, isn't she?"

"She can be," I agreed. "We used to date."

"Oh, Ben," she said, pausing to touch my arm. "I didn't mean to offend you."

"Please, you'll have to try a lot harder than that. There's nobody in Harper's Landing who knows just how scary she can be better than me. I'll be happy to act as your listening board as you organize your thoughts, if you'd like."

"Thanks, I appreciate that."

As we walked on, she said, "I guess the first place to start is with Barry Hill."

"I've never heard of him," I admitted. "Who is he?"

"Barry is, I guess I should start getting used to saying *was*, Connie's fiancé. It ended badly last month, and he refused to accept it. Lately he's gotten kind of dark in his phone messages to her, and to be honest with you, he scares me."

"Is there any chance he's in town right now?" The man certainly sounded like a viable suspect, and at the moment I was in dire need of one or two that weren't my girlfriend.

"Who knows where Barry is at any time of the day or night? He's independently wealthy, so he comes and goes as he pleases. That's one of the reasons Connie broke up with him."

"Because he was rich?" I'd heard a lot of excuses in my life, but never that a prospective spouse had too much money.

"No, because he had no purpose in his life." She stopped a second, then added, "You didn't know Connie, and I'm willing to bet she made a horrid first impression on you."

"I thought she was a little self-aggrandizing," I admitted. "That sounded harsh, didn't it? I shouldn't be speaking ill of the dead like that."

"She wouldn't have minded, believe me. Connie was always a straight talker. I'm willing to bet that what you took for arrogance was probably just that she was always a nervous wreck whenever she had to speak in public. She hated it, to be honest with you."

"Then why did she agree to come here?" I'd heard Diana tell enough stories about authors with tremendous stage fright, but that always centered around folks who wrote fiction. This woman was a soapmaker who happened to write books, so giving demonstrations while she spoke should have been second nature to her.

"She came to Harper's Landing for a particular reason," Sharon admitted. "And it wasn't just your Soap Celebration. But I'm not ready to talk about that yet."

"Why not?" I asked.

"Ben," she said as she stopped and stared at me, "there are some secrets I won't divulge, not until I truly believe it is the last resort."

"Sorry, I didn't mean to push you about it," I said. "Who's on your list besides Mr. Hill?"

"There's a woman named Betsy Blair I think the police should investigate. I happen to know she's in town, and she certainly thought she had reason to hate Connie, though it was all in her head."

"Why did she hate her?" It amazed me that so many people had the energy to hate this woman so passionately, and yet Sharon kept defending her; I had to believe there had been at least some good in the soapmaker.

"She claims Connie stole her latest book out from under her. There's no merit in the accusation. This Blair woman sent Connie a manuscript, and somehow she managed to do it without going through me. I would have thrown it away in a heartbeat without replying, but Connie made the mistake of sending an encouraging letter back to her. She hated to snuff out a fellow soapmaker's hopes.

"Anyway, the woman filed suit. With Connie's letter and the supposed similarities in the manuscripts, there's enough to make it look legitimate, on first glance. Betsy was here last night, tagging along with the man who served us the papers."

"Is it possible there's any merit to her claim?"

Sharon shook her head. "There's no way. Connie wouldn't show me the manuscript, but she did hold on to it, just in case. She said it was full of rambling tangents and pitiful instructions. Betsy didn't even use photos. There are drawings illustrating the process, and from the way Connie described them to me, they're as bad as the writing."

"Surely a judge would see that as well."

Sharon shrugged. "That's what Connie told her when they served the papers, and Betsy went ballistic. She started screaming that she'd get even, and the server had to drag her off himself. She made quite a scene. If you ask me, she's not at all in her right mind."

We'd walked several blocks and were now standing in front of the Hound Dog Café. Ruby, the woman who ran it, was a self-proclaimed Elvis Presley nut, and the furnishings and music backed up the claim.

"Could we stop in here and get some sweet tea?" Sharon asked. "All this talking has made me thirsty."

"Sure," I said, eager to keep her chatting. The more Sharon said, the more reasons I had to give Molly that Diana hadn't killed the soapmaker.

Ruby greeted us with a nod, not saying a word as we walked to a booth in back. I wondered about the silent treatment, and then realized that she was a big fan of Diana's, and it looked as though I might be stepping out on her in her direst time of need. I planned to tell Ruby that I would never do that when she came to take our order, but she resolutely ignored us.

"Is service always this bad here?" Sharon asked. "We could go somewhere else."

"Hang on a second," I said. "I'll be right back."

I approached Ruby, who pretended to be cleaning the counter in front of her. She must have gone over the same spot a dozen times since we'd come in.

"Ruby, when you get the chance, we need two sweet teas."

"How's Diana?" she asked, ignoring my request.

"She's in trouble," I admitted. "That's why I'm trying to interview the assistant to the woman who was murdered. I can't help Diana a bit by sitting around hoping Molly finds the killer on her own. Give me a hand here, will you? Sharon just lost a boss and a dear friend, Diana's the number one suspect, and I'm trying to figure out who did it." Maybe calling her boss "a dear friend" was stretching it, but I was going for sympathy.

"I've got you now," Ruby said as she nodded. "I'll be right over as soon as I get the chance."

I walked back to the table, then explained, "We're all set."

Twenty seconds later, Ruby approached with a tray holding more than just tea.

"Do you like pie?" she asked Sharon.

"I love it," she said, clearly a little confused by the question.

Ruby slid a piece of lemon meringue pie in front of her. "You should try this."

"Hey, I didn't order any pie," I said.

"Don't worry, you're not getting any. This is for your guest."

And Ruby was gone before I could protest.

Sharon shoved the plate toward me. "You can have it, Ben. I don't feel much like eating."

I glanced over to see that Ruby was still watching us pretty closely. In a soft voice, I said, "If I eat that pie, she'll never forgive me. You'd better take a bite before she throws us both out."

"You can't be serious."

"Sharon, turn around and see if I'm lying."

She did, and saw Ruby's glance. "This town is odd, isn't it?"

"You don't know the half of it."

Sharon put a small bite on her fork, then said, "Once I taste it, you can have the rest." She ate the morsel of pie, smiled suddenly, then had another bite.

"Hey, what happened to my portion?"

Sharon took another bite, then said, "I'm sure she's got more back there. I'm not sharing." It was the first smile I'd seen on Sharon's face all day, and I was thankful that Ruby had done exactly the right thing by bringing her pie.

I winked at her when Sharon wasn't looking, and soon enough I had my own piece of pie, this one apple crisp.

"How is that?" Ruby asked Sharon as she slid the plate in front of me.

"It's the best pie I've ever had in my life," Sharon said.

I swear I nearly dropped my fork as Ruby actually blushed at the compliment. "I'm glad you like it."

"I do," Sharon said.

Ruby faded away, and I took a bite from my own slice. As I chewed it, I noticed that Sharon was watching me.

"That looks good," she said.

"It really is," I said, savoring another bite.

"Don't I get a taste?"

I looked at the remnants of lemon meringue on her plate. "I don't know, you weren't willing to share with me." I smiled as I said it, cutting my piece down the middle and giving her half.

"I suppose I could part with one bite," she said as she started to section off what was left of her slice.

"I was just teasing," I said. "If I wanted any, I'd order a piece for myself."

Sharon dug into the apple, then said, "I'm taking some of these home with me when I go."

"How long are you going to stay?" I asked.

Her smile suddenly vanished. "You know what? I don't have any idea. As soon as I talk to the police about my list of suspects, I'll move out of the bed-and-breakfast, though. It must be costing you a fortune, and I don't need anything that nice."

"We don't mind," I said, realizing that I was going to have to talk long and hard to get my mother to agree to picking up the bill for an extended stay.

"No, I couldn't," she said. "We saw a motel on the way into town. It's called the Mountain Lake or Lake Mountain or something like that. I'd be just as happy out there. Happier, if you want to know the truth. I've never been a big fan of bed-and-breakfasts, though Connie always insisted we stay in them whenever we traveled. It feels too much like I'm someone's houseguest. I'd rather be alone."

"I'll help you move myself," I said.

"That won't be necessary. I'm used to packing often when we're traveling."

The front door of the diner opened, and Molly walked in. She started to order a cup of coffee, then saw Sharon and me sitting in back.

"I want that to go, Ruby," she said as she approached us.

"I was just looking for you," she said.

"I've been right here," I replied.

"I'm not talking to you."

I decided to ignore the frost in her voice and add a little of my own. "I don't care, you're talking to me now. Do you still have Diana locked up?"

Molly looked at me and shook her head. "Do you ever get tired, jumping to conclusions like you do all the time? Diana was never under arrest, and you know it."

"You wanted to question her after her medical exam though, didn't you?"

"Ben, whether you like it or not, that's part of my job. She and Kelly came by my office awhile ago, but neither one of them had much to say. Frankly, I wasn't at all satisfied with her answers."

"Maybe she didn't care for your questions," I said.

Sharon looked uncomfortable. "Should I excuse myself?"

Before I could reply, Molly said, "No, Ben's finished." She stared at me, then added, "You know you're not why I'm here."

"I'd tell you how much that admission hurts my feelings, but I doubt I could carry it off convincingly."

Molly ignored the remark as she looked at Sharon and said, "I'd like to go through your employer's things in her room, if you don't mind."

"I'm happy to do whatever I can to help," she said as she got up. "We're staying at Jean Henshaw's B&B."

"I know," Molly said. "I was hoping you might be able to give me some insights into the woman as I search."

"I'm happy to help in whatever way I can," Sharon said.

"Your coffee's ready," Ruby called out.

Molly asked Sharon, "Are you coming?"

"Give me one second," she replied, then Sharon turned to me. "Thanks, Ben, for everything."

"Hey, I just ordered the tea. Ruby brought the pie on her own."

"You know what I'm talking about," she said, "and it's got nothing to do with dessert. You're a good listener."

"I'm just happy I could help." I lowered my voice to a whisper and asked, "Are you ready to talk to her now?"

"I think so," Sharon said.

"You'll feel a lot better once you do," I said. "Give Molly a chance. She might be tough, but she's usually fair, and she's also the best cop I've ever known in my life."

"You can actually say that with a straight face after what I just heard?"

"We bicker all the time," I admitted. "We've been doing it since grade school."

"Well, you're both very good at it. It must be all that practice."

"Listen, I meant what I said. Tell her everything. You can trust her."

"Okay, I will," she said.

Molly must have overheard some of what I'd said, because she smiled at me as they left. I was glad we were back on familiar footing. There had been some turbulent times in our relationship lately, and it had bothered me a great deal more than I'd been willing to admit. When all was said and done, Molly was my very best friend, though I never would have admitted it to anyone in the world, especially her.

Ruby slid the bill under my plate, and I saw it was just for the tea. "Hey, we had pie, too."

No one else was in the café at the moment, but she still lowered her voice as she said, "That was on me, and if you tell anybody in town, I'll call you a liar to your face."

"Hey, my lips are sealed," I said. I slid a tip under my glass that was more than enough to cover the pie, too. Ruby would fuss at me for doing it—I knew her well enough to realize that—but I didn't mind. It was part of living in a small town, the give-and-take in the art of getting along, an ability that was highly prized in Harper's Landing.

As I walked back to Where There's Soap, I suddenly realized something. Sharon had been so convincing in naming two suspects besides Diana, I'd nearly forgotten that she'd left one out.

Sharon herself could have had more reason than anyone else to want her employer dead. Were the other people she mentioned legitimate suspects, or was Sharon just trying to divert suspicion away from herself? Whatever the reason, I knew Molly was too good a cop not to consider that angle as well.

Still, I was going to do a little digging of my own, especially considering that Diana was probably still Molly's number one suspect.

UNFORTUNATELY, my amateur detection would have to wait. I found my family gathered in the front area of the soap shop, and a table and chairs from the break room that I'd helped put up earlier were back where they had been this morning. My family was gathered around, and all of them looked expectantly at me as I walked in. It was after our regular business hours, but just barely. Still, I'd expected to find my family scattered throughout Harper's Landing instead of clustered together like a handful of marbles.

As I studied them, I said, "Aren't we digressing here? I could swear I helped put that table away earlier."

"Where have you been?" Mom asked.

She usually gave me some leeway in my job, so I was surprised by her tone of voice. "I've been detecting," I said as I tapped my forehead. "It's brutal work, but I'm throwing myself into it."

"And did you discover anything?"

"I can say one thing, without fear of contradiction. Ruby makes . . . one of the best pies in Harper's Landing." I'd almost said the best, but I'd caught it just in time. My mother is prouder of her baked goods than she is of me on most days, and I would have paid dearly for the comment.

Jim whistled, then said, "Nice save, Bro."

He was the only one who'd dared to talk, and one withering glare from our mother was enough to silence him.

"Did you manage to come to any other conclusions while you were gone?" she asked.

"Listen, what's going on? Did I miss a memo or something? I didn't know we were having a family meeting. What's on the agenda?"

I'd been joking, but Kate said, "If you ever read your e-mail, you'd know."

"Hey, I just figured out how to turn my computer on yesterday. Do you honestly expect me to get on the Internet? Besides, I'm always here. Why didn't you just say something to me earlier?"

Kate flushed. "Because I just asked for this meeting. It's the perfect time for us to add to our offerings, and I want to make my pitch to everyone at one time."

We had a rule in our family. Though normally it was run as a benevolent tyranny by our mother, Mom did allow us to pitch the entire family on new ideas for our business. It was an inquisition most of us wouldn't go through willingly, but when one of the kids had a new idea, it got a fair trial from the rest of us.

"Sorry, I didn't mean to interfere with your presentation." I took a seat next to Cindy, who whispered, "You're late."

I smiled. "It's a real tragedy, isn't it?"

She tweaked my arm. "Ben, don't you take anything seriously?"

"I try not to. It adds too many worry lines, and my face has enough as it is without any outside help."

Kate coughed once, and I shut my mouth. It was hard enough to make a presentation without whispering going on in the crowd, and my family was murder about karma. The next time I pitched something, Kate would bring in a marching band if I made too much noise for her taste in this presentation.

I tried to look encouraging and attentive as I gave her my full consideration. It was the least she deserved.

Glancing at a stack of note cards, Kate nodded to herself, then made eye contact with each of us as she spoke. "I feel it's time we expand our basic line from just the soaps we carry now to a wide range of beauty and stress-relieving products."

There were a few murmurs among my brothers and sisters. The Perkins clan had been in the soap business, and just the soap business, for generations. It was a dramatic proposal indeed.

Kate went on, speaking over the doubters. "We need to drag ourselves into the twenty-first century. There are so many complementary products we should be carrying that fit perfectly with our carefully and lovingly handcrafted soap."

I raised a hand, an acceptable form of questioning. Kate looked reluctant to call on me, but I didn't back down, and she finally acknowledged me. No doubt she was expecting a blast, since I was known as one of the more traditional members of our family. I was a man of limited interests, devoting my life to the craft of soapmaking, and I could see how she might think I'd believe it heresy to branch out.

"What products did you have in mind, and are they things we can make here ourselves?"

She, along with the rest of my family, appeared to be shocked to hear an intelligent question coming from me.

"I'm glad you asked, Ben. I believe we should start small, with just a few products that we can easily fabricate ourselves. In addition, there are kits available from some of our suppliers."

"That's all well and good, but what exactly are you talking about?"

I'd forgotten to raise my hand, but nobody commented on it. Kate held up a display that she'd obviously spent a great deal of time on.

"In the beginning, I think we should add lip balms and hand lotions, but at a later date, I'd like to add bath salts and fizzies to our line."

I nodded. "I think it's a wonderful idea."

"Benjamin, I didn't see your hand," Mom said, though I could tell that she approved of my statements.

"Look closer, Mom, they're both right here," I said as I waved them in the air.

That got a chuckle from most of my family, but not my mother. "Are you finished with your tomfoolery? Kate has more to tell us."

"I can't make any promises, but I'll try," I said.

Kate grinned at me, but she cut it short as our mother returned her attention to the front.

She continued, "Making these products is in many ways similar to what we do now. We'll go over the processes later, but initially, I'd like you all to approve a Spa Indulgence corner of the sales floor. I think a six-month test would be fair, and I'd like to get started on it immediately."

She sat down in a nearby chair, and I could see the presentation had been a strain for her. Kate was wonderful one-on-one, but she was uncomfortable speaking in front of groups, even if she happened to be related to the entire audience.

I raised my hand. "I have some questions about profit margins on small runs in back and sales up here. Have you done any kind of financial breakdown on your proposal?"

Kate nodded. "I've done cost-benefit analyses on everything, and we can actually make more money on these new items than we do on soap."

That got a few nods from the crowd. We all kept a careful watch on our business bottom line, and if anything could add to it, most of us would be in favor of it.

"How about the materials? What are we going to have to carry that we don't already have?"

"We can get our needed supplies from John Labott," Kate said as she nodded toward Louisa. "He's giving us a very good deal on our materials."

And why shouldn't he, since he'd been dating Louisa for some time?

"Are there any other questions?" Kate asked.

"Where would you like to put it?" Mom asked sternly. She guarded the store's layout with a vengeance, and I knew that would be the hardest part of Kate's sale.

She stood and walked to the corner between the break room and the outer wall. It was the least desirable floor space in the shop. "We could put it right here."

"Nonsense," Mom said. "That would never work. It's where I have the clearance section. Do you have any other ideas?"

"Not just yet," Kate asked. "I wanted to see what you all thought of the basic idea first."

"Very well," Mom said. "If there are no other questions, we will vote. In order of your ages, come into the break room and fill out a ballot. *Yes* means you approve of the idea, *no* means the opposite. Any questions?"

I started to say something sarcastic, but I buried it when I saw the tension on Kate's face.

No one else said anything either. "Let's vote."

The second Mom walked into the break room, my siblings gathered around Kate to congratulate her on her presentation.

Mom popped out a second later. "Benjamin? It's your turn."

I went into the break room and wrote *yes* in bold letters.

Five minutes later, we'd all voted, and Mom said, "I'll be right back."

She was as good as her word, but when she rejoined us, there was a stern look on her face. Kate's expression died the second she saw it.

Mom announced, "We have a decision. Congratulations, Kate. You've got your space."

We all celebrated with her until Mom held up one hand. "There's just one problem, as I see it."

"What's that?" Kate asked, her enthusiasm tempered for a moment.

"Since the back area clearly won't do, I'd like to propose we give your idea a fair trial and make room toward the front of the shop. Do you have any objections?"

For a second Kate was nine years old. She hugged Mom and said, "Thank you. Thank you all."

We applauded, and Mom said, "I expect to see your layout before you touch a single item on our shelves. Agreed?"

"Absolutely," Kate said.

Mom nodded, then said, "The meeting is adjourned."

We were all feeling pretty good about our family and our business when the phone rang. Louisa just happened to be standing nearby, so she picked it up, despite the fact that we were officially closed.

"Ben, it's for you," she said over the chatter of our family.

"Take a message," I said. "This calls for champagne."

"I think you're going to want to take this call," she said, and I felt my heart sink. I had no idea who wanted to talk to me, but from the look on Louisa's face, there was little doubt in my mind that I wasn't going to like it.

FIVE

∘ ∘ ∘

"**THIS** is Ben Perkins," I said, after getting a quizzical look from Louisa. Why was she staring at me like that? She had to know more about who was on the telephone than I did, since she was the one who had just answered it.

"Am I interrupting anything?" a familiar voice asked.

"Hi, Kelly. No, we're just handling some family business. What can I do for you?"

"Ben, we need to talk," she said.

"If it's about Diana, I already ran into Molly. She said your meeting today didn't go particularly well. Good job."

"Ben, you know I can't talk to you about one of my clients."

"Then what did you want to talk about?" She certainly had my curiosity up.

Kelly hesitated, then said, "I can't do this over the phone. Are you free tonight?"

"What about your daughter?" I asked, not mentioning

her ex-husband Wade's name. Kelly had broken up with me to reconcile with him, though I'd heard enough rumors around town that it wasn't working out. I had been upset losing Kelly, and then Diana had come into my life. Still, I had enough feelings left for Kelly to feel my heart skip just a little at the sound of her voice, even though I was firmly committed to Diana.

"Annie and Wade are having dinner together," Kelly admitted. "I don't suppose you'd like to get a bite with me, would you?"

"Sorry, but I've got plans with Diana," I said, not trying to be hurtful in any way.

"I understand," Kelly said, a little more curtly than I liked. "Would you have time to meet me afterward, then?"

I glanced at my watch. "I'm not picking her up for an hour, so if you've got the time, I can meet you now. Should I come by your office?"

"How did you know where I was?" she asked. "Have you been keeping tabs on me?"

"No, I just figured that's where you would be." I'd driven past her law office several times lately, at all hours of the day and night, and more often than not, Kelly's car was parked out front. I didn't know when she had time for Annie, but then I realized that really wasn't any of my business anymore.

"I'll see you in five minutes," I added.

"I'll be waiting for you."

After I hung up the phone, I started toward the door, but Louisa cut me off. "What was that all about?"

"What are you talking about? Can't a man be friends with an old girlfriend?"

"She hasn't had that status long," Louisa said. "Ben, you're not going to do something stupid, are you?"

"I rarely plan those kinds of things in advance," I said, trying to lighten the tone of our conversation. We were starting to attract some attention from our other family members, and I hated to be in their crosshairs, especially tonight.

"I mean it," she said. "You need to be careful."

"I will," I said, then I stopped and kissed Kate on the cheek on my way out. "Congratulations, Sis, you did a fine job."

"I was scared to death, and you know it," she said. "But thanks for your vote."

"How do you know I voted yes?" I asked her.

"Because I'd kill you if you didn't."

I laughed. "My pencil nearly pierced the ballot, I pressed down so heard on that *y*."

"So where are you off to? Stay and celebrate with us."

"I'd love to, but I've got an appointment."

"This late in the day?" Kate asked as she glanced at her watch. "Are you sure you can't put it off until tomorrow?"

"From the sound of things, it won't wait," I said as I ducked out without any more explanations. As I drove my Miata to Kelly's office, I couldn't help wondering what she wanted to talk about. Even though I knew I'd find out soon enough, that still didn't keep me from speculating on a thousand different possibilities as I drove to her office.

"THANKS for coming by on such short notice, Ben," Kelly said as I walked in.

"I'd be lying if I said I wasn't curious about your summons. What's going on?"

"Right to the heart of the matter. That's one of the things I like best about you." Her voice softened as she added, "You seem happy."

"I can't imagine how. It's more than a little disturbing to have someone killed in my shop. When you consider that Diana is tied in with the victim, I'd say all and all I'm pretty miserable at the moment."

"I meant before today," she added haltingly.

What did she expect me to say? "Kelly, I'm sorry for everything that happened between us."

She looked at me as if I'd slapped her. "I'm not. I enjoyed spending time with you. I just wish . . ."

I couldn't believe I was having this conversation with her. "You know I did, too. That's not what I meant. I should have said how sorry I was about how things ended. I guess we both just wanted different things. Please tell me that's not why you called me this evening."

She shrugged her shoulders slightly, then looked carefully at me as she asked, "You're digging into this woman's murder, aren't you?"

"Whatever gave you that idea?" I replied as innocently as I could manage.

She laughed. "Come on, Ben, I haven't known you forever like just about everyone else in Harper's Landing has, but I know you can't pass this up, especially with what's at stake."

"Okay, I'll admit that I've been giving it some thought, but there's nothing wrong with that, is there?"

"Not as far as I'm concerned." She picked a brass paperweight up off her desk, shifted it from hand to hand, then put it back down. "What I'm about to share with you is idle speculation, nothing more. I've mentioned it to Molly, but I'm afraid she's not being as zealous as either one of us would like."

"And you think I will be? I'm a soapmaker first and foremost, not a detective."

Kelly smiled. "Ben, this isn't your first mix-up with murder. You've proven to have good instincts when it comes to these matters, and I don't doubt you can be of assistance now. But if you'd rather not know what I suspect, I'll apologize for bothering you and you can be on your way."

I wasn't about to get up from that seat until she told me what she had to say, and we both knew it. It was time to cut to the chase, though.

"Okay, I'm listening."

"Then you admit you're investigating this Brown woman's homicide?"

She was baiting me now. "Kelly, I'm not a hostile witness on the stand. I admit it."

That got an instant look of contrition from her. "I'm sorry. I've been dragging this out, haven't I? I suspect that I've been a little lonely lately, and I'm taking advantage of you."

How could she be lonely? She had a daughter and a husband at home with her. I wasn't about to get into that with her, though. While we were still cordial toward each other, we'd both treated the subject of our past as a forbidden topic of conversation up until now.

She paused, then said, "I suspect one of Molly's fellow police officers is a little more involved in this case than she's willing to acknowledge."

She certainly knew how to get my attention.

"What makes you say that?"

Kelly leaned forward in her chair. "I've had some dealings in Fiddler's Gap that might be a factor in this case. While I don't doubt for an instant that Molly's sources here in town are broader reaching than mine, I doubt she has the connections in other areas I do. What do you know about Fiddler's Gap?"

"I haven't spent much time there, besides going to Krankle's Bakery." Kelly had introduced me to the odd but sweet old couple, and I'd been going there whenever I had the chance ever since. It was one of those family businesses that gave small towns part of their charm.

"They're on vacation for the next six weeks, did you know that? Anyway, I was up there a few months ago, and I got into a conversation with Gustav about a customer of his who left as I was coming in. The man looked vaguely familiar, but I didn't know his name. Anyway, you know how Gustav likes to talk, so he started telling me about the man. He said he'd been jilted at the altar twenty years ago, and it had soured him on love. It took me a few weeks to realize where I'd seen him before, and then it came to me. His name's Brian Ross, and he's a cop right here in Harper's Landing."

"Our town isn't that big. Are you trying to tell me that you had a hard time figuring out who he was?"

"It's all about context, Ben. He was out of uniform, and in a town I didn't associate him with. That's not the point."

"I've been wondering if there was one," I said.

She laughed. "I've missed your sense of humor, too."

What could I say to that? *Thanks* didn't seem like an appropriate response, so I just waited as patiently as I could.

Finally, Kelly explained, "I didn't give Ross another thought until today. That's when I heard a name again that Gustav had told me."

"The name of the would-be bride," I said.

"Yes."

"It was Connie Brown," I said, suddenly knowing it in my heart.

Kelly nodded her approval. "I told you that you were good at this."

"He was at the shop today with all of the other cops Molly called in," I admitted. "Do you honestly believe he could have held a grudge that long and killed her when he got the opportunity?"

"Molly clearly doesn't think of it as a possibility," Kelly said. "But it bears looking into, don't you think?"

"How in the world am I going to ask a cop questions about his alibi? It's not an easy thing to do for somebody who's not in law enforcement."

"Use your imagination, Ben. You said yourself he was working today, so that puts him at the scene. Have they found the murder weapon yet?"

"The first guess made at the scene was that the murderer used a hammer, but they're not sure yet."

Kelly nodded. "If it was a hammer, that would make it an easily accessible weapon. So we've got motive, means, and opportunity."

I nodded. "We've got those for Diana, too."

Kelly said, "True, but we know Diana didn't do it."

"By the way, I never thanked you for taking on her case. I really do appreciate it."

She frowned. "I seem to have a hard time saying no to you, don't I? Is your mother pressuring you to solve this, too?"

I was about to answer when her phone rang. "Sorry, it's the private line. I have to get it."

"Go ahead."

I had a lot to think about as Kelly answered her phone. I knew Molly had a soft spot in her heart for her fellow police officers, but I couldn't imagine her turning a blind eye to murder; she was too good a cop to do that.

I was still thinking about the possibilities when I heard Kelly say angrily, "I'll be there when you see me. For once you have to wait on *me*." She started to slam the phone down, but I saw her check the motion and slowly cradle it.

I started to stand. "I'll let you go," I said. "I appreciate the information. I'm just not sure what I can do about it."

"You don't have to leave," Kelly said.

I glanced at my watch. "Honestly, I do. We both have other places we need to be. Thanks for the tip."

"You're welcome," she said.

As I walked out of her office, I realized all was not bliss at the Sheer household. Kelly had known she'd be in for some rocky times when she and her husband had decided to try again, and I felt bad for her, but I had problems of my own. It had been wonderful talking to her again, having a real conversation not filled with undertones of tension between us. It was easy to see why I'd been so intrigued by her. After all, she was smart, funny, and beautiful. Unfortunately, she had also been unavailable to me. I was happy with Diana, always glad to be in her presence, and I wouldn't let anything spoil that if I could help it. The two women were so much alike in so many ways. I tended to gravitate toward strong, smart women, and Diana and Kelly were both that.

I glanced at my watch and saw that if I didn't hurry, I was going to be late for my date.

I had to ring her bell twice before Diana came to the door. It was clear from the redness in her eyes that she'd been crying. Normally dressed to perfection, Diana wore baggy gray sweatpants and an old jersey with West Virginia University's logo on it.

"Hi, Ben," she said as she dabbed at her eyes. "I'm sorry, I should have called you. I can't do this tonight."

"If you want to be alone, I fully understand."

She shook her head. "It's not that. I just don't have the heart to face the world. Look at me."

"I think you look great," I said, and I meant it.

"You're sweet, but you're also a really bad liar."

I took her in my arms and kissed her. After thirty seconds, I pulled away and said, "Do you still think I'm lying?"

"You're starting to convince me," she said.

"Hey, was that a smile? Tell you what; I don't feel like facing the world either. Why don't I go pick up a pizza and we can watch an old movie together."

"I don't feel like changing," she said.

"Then don't do it on my account. I happen to like the way you look."

She shook her head. "Then you're delusional. I appreciate the offer, honestly I do, but I need to be by myself tonight."

"Are you sure? I'd be happy to spend the evening with you. If it's the pizza you don't want, we could have some barbeque instead."

She shoved me toward the door. "No, it's not the menu or the companionship. I just want to take a long, hot soak in my tub and then go to sleep. Do you mind?"

I kissed her again, this time more briefly than before. "Whatever you want," I said.

"Thanks for understanding."

"Do I have much choice?" I asked, adding a smile.

"Not tonight. Call me tomorrow, okay?"

"First thing," I said as I walked away. I suddenly had a free evening. So what was I going to do about it? Was it too late to talk to Brian Ross? Had Molly learned anything yet about the murder weapon? I decided I'd talk to her first, then see if I could feel her out about her coworker, and the chance he'd held a bad grudge all these years and had finally done something about it. Sharon still had some of my attention as a suspect, no matter how convincing she was at playing the part of mourning employee. There was also the matter of Betsy Blair. Could she have killed Connie in a fit of rage, honestly believing that her manuscript had been stolen? Finally, there was the latest fiancé, the mysterious Barry Hill. It would help if I knew if he was in town, but I didn't have the resources to check. Then I realized that it would just take a few telephone calls to find out. There weren't that many places to stay in Harper's Landing, and if Hill was anything like his onetime fiancé, I had a feeling he'd go only with the best we had to offer.

There was a lot to talk to Molly about, but I wasn't sure she'd want to hear any of it from me.

Still, I owed her the chance to respond, and maybe I'd even manage to help her in her investigation. Though she hated to admit it, in the past I'd given Molly a piece or two of the puzzles she'd been working on, so maybe she'd be more receptive than I expected.

But I doubted it.

I found Molly at her desk in police headquarters, searching through a stack of papers that buried the top of it. She was dressed in her police uniform, and her hair was pulled back in a tight bun, though a few strands of her hair had managed to escape.

"You're working too hard," I said.

When she looked up, Molly seemed surprised to see me. "What are you doing here? And how did you get back to the bullpen?"

"Nobody was at the front desk, so I just walked on back," I admitted.

"That desk is supposed to be manned twenty-four hours a day," Molly snapped.

"Sorry I bothered you," I said as I started to retreat. "I'll go back out front and wait." Molly was clearly in no mood for my input, so the best thing I could do was beat a hasty retreat and try her again when she was feeling more receptive.

"You're not actually going to walk back to the front desk and wait for me to come get you, are you?"

"Molly, I can see that you're busy. We can talk another time."

She shoved her chair away from the desk. "Ben, I'm always busy. We don't have the budget to hire as many cops as we need, so that means we all have to pitch in to clear things up."

"Hey, I get it."

Again I tried to leave, but she wouldn't let me. "Okay, stop being so understanding. You're making me nervous."

I shrugged. "What can I say? It's the new me. See you later."

I was at the Miata outside when I heard her calling my name. "Ben, hang on a second."

I waited for her, then as she approached, I said, "If I knew playing hard-to-get worked on you, I would have used it a long time ago."

She grinned. "To be honest with you, I'd grab just about any excuse to get away from that avalanche of paperwork in there. It's getting so bad, we have to document it every time we go to the john. Now seriously, what's up?"

"I was hoping to buy you a cup of coffee and talk to you about the murder today," I said.

I was expecting a blast from her, and no doubt I deserved it for meddling in police business, but to my surprise, she said, "Yeah, I'd like that."

"My thoughts?"

"No, the coffee. And dinner, while you're at it. I'm hungry. Come on, take me for a spin in this thing. You know how much I love riding in your convertible."

"The salesman was right," I said as I held the door open for her. "This thing's a chick magnet."

"Only if they have steel plates in their heads," Molly said.

As I got in, I asked, "So, where do you want to go?"

"How about The Hound Dog?" she suggested. "I could go for some pie, too, as long as you're buying."

"On one condition," I said. "You have to at least appear to be interested in what I have to say. I don't care if you listen or not, just nod between bites, okay?"

"I could probably manage that," she admitted. "I feigned interest in your conversations every time we went out."

"You can't fool me," I said as I pulled out. "You were always riveted to whatever I had to say."

"See? It worked."

"Tell you what," I said as I drove. "Why don't I start telling you what I've found out so far while we drive? That way it won't spoil your meal."

"You're not about to do that," she said.

"What, start talking now?"

"No, spoil my dinner break. Ruby's offerings deserve the utmost of my attention."

I laughed. "You never change, do you?"

"I wouldn't say that," she said. "I think I've grown quite a bit lately. Your brother is good for me."

"Tell me the truth," I said, forgetting for a minute why

I'd come by. We were talking as old friends now, and the murder wasn't a part of the conversation. "Did you ever, in your wildest dreams, suspect you'd date my little brother?"

"No, we've talked about that. I've got a feeling he was interested in me long before I returned the favor."

"Are you kidding me? He's had a crush on you since he saw me take you to the senior prom. You did look pretty spectacular that night."

"Yeah, well, you clean up pretty good yourself. I'd ask you about your love life, but I only have forty-five minutes for my break."

"You're right, that's nowhere near enough time."

I pulled into a parking spot in front of the café, and Molly waited patiently for me to get her door. It wasn't a matter of strength or subjugation; it was simply a courtesy. Good manners were still strong in our part of the South.

There were a few people in the diner, but lunch was Ruby's busiest time of day, and breakfast was second, leaving the evening meal a distant third.

As we walked in, I asked her, "Ruby, why do you stay open for dinner? It can't be worth your while."

"That depends on how you look at it," she said with a smile. "What else am I going to do, watch television? No thanks, this is where I belong."

Molly poked me in the ribs. "And we're glad you're here."

We found a booth away from everyone else, and Molly studied the menu. I knew what I wanted.

When Ruby showed up with two iced teas, unasked for but deeply appreciated, she said, "You two want your usual meals?"

Molly nodded. "Yeah, but make it a double cheeseburger

instead of a single, bring me an order of fries with my onion rings, and I'll have a slice of pie later."

"So you're buying," she said as she looked at me. "Does that mean you'll be having a salad?"

"You can bring one if you want, but I'm just going to sneer at it. I'll have country-style steak, mashed potatoes and gravy, and cooked apples. Put a biscuit on top and I'll be a happy man."

"Watch out for the big spender, everybody," Ruby said, smiling. She loved it when her customers ordered a lot of food, and not just for the cash register. Ruby loved feeding people, and she said she always figured the more they ate, the happier it made her. "You want pie with that, too?"

"Make it strawberry cobbler," I said, "and you've got yourself a deal."

She laughed as she made her way back to the kitchen. "Get ready, Garnet, we've got a couple of big eaters here."

"I'm ready," her cook said.

As we waited for our food, Molly took a sip of tea, then said, "Ben, I'm working on an active police investigation, so I can't exactly share any information with you. In fact, I really shouldn't listen to anything you might have to say concerning the homicide today."

I started to protest when she held up a hand. "However, if you decide to talk anyway, I can insist right now that I'm not listening, so as far as official police business goes, you're wasting your breath."

"That's fine with me. Here's who I suspect so far." I went through my list, saving her fellow cop for last. I strongly suspected that would be the one point she wouldn't let me slide on, and I was right. We were nearly finished with our meals when his name finally came into the conversation.

"And then there's Brian Ross," I casually dropped into our conversation.

Molly waved a french fry in my face. "Not you, too. I don't even have to ask you where you got that nonsense, do I? Kelly Sheer's been putting ideas into your head."

"He's got to be considered a legitimate suspect," I said, "even if he is a cop."

"Lower your voice," Molly commanded. "I'm not stupid, Ben. I looked into Brian's whereabouts when the murder occurred. He was on the other side of town the entire time."

"Is there anyone who can confirm that?" I asked.

"You're wrong about him, Ben. Drop it."

I put my fork down. "Molly, you have to treat him like everybody else. You're too good a cop to do otherwise."

"This conversation is over," she said as she stood.

"Hey, what about your pie?"

"I've lost my appetite," she said. "Thanks for dinner."

She walked out of the restaurant, and I threw a twenty on the table. "Thanks, Ruby," I called out as I started to leave.

"What about dessert?"

"Not tonight. Don't worry about change. I put a twenty-dollar bill on the table. You and Garnet have our dessert yourselves, okay?"

Molly was outside, still steaming from my supposition.

When she saw me exit, she smiled faintly. "It's hard to make a dramatic exit when I need a ride back to the station."

I nodded, not saying a word as I held the car door open for her. We rode back in silence, and I realized that I'd pushed her a little further than she'd been willing to take. Still, if I planted a single seed of doubt in her mind about

Brian Ross, it would be worth it. All I wanted was for her to focus on the other suspects in the case besides Diana.

When we got back to the station, she finally spoke. "Thanks for the meal."

"You're most welcome," I said as I started to get out.

She popped the door open and got out. "Don't bother."

I couldn't even protest.

Molly started to walk back to the station, then stopped and came back toward my car.

She leaned down to my open window and said, "He didn't do it, I know that in my heart, but I'll look into it."

"That's all I ask," I said.

"I'd tell you to drop this, but I know you won't. Just don't do anything stupid, all right?"

I looked at her a second, then said, "I'll try, but then that's always my goal. Is there anything you can tell me that I don't already know?"

She hesitated, then finally said, "I'm going to regret this, and if you tell anybody I told you, I'll lock you up out of pure spite."

"I'll keep my mouth shut; it's a deal."

"We found the murder weapon. There were no prints on it, but there was enough evidence on it for us to know we got the right hammer. By the way, it's one of yours."

"Mine?" I wasn't even sure I owned a hammer anymore.

"Not yours. I mean it belongs to your shop. It was in your Dumpster in back, so whoever killed her tossed it in there as they left the property."

"At least that's what they want you to think," I said.

"For the record, if anyone asks, we're pursuing leads actively on several fronts." She shook her head as she walked away and added, "Good night, Ben."

"Good night," I called out to her. "And thanks."

I'd done what I'd set out to do, so why didn't I feel better about where things stood in the investigation? Maybe it was because I had to count on Molly and not do it myself.

There were at least a few things I could still do tonight, though, and I was determined to keep digging.

SIX

∘ ∘ ∘

"I'M not asking for much. I just need to know if you have a man named Barry Hill staying here."

The clerk in front of me was no more helpful than he'd been on the phone when I'd called the Lakefront Inn earlier. I'd decided the best way to get information was face-to-face, but clearly I'd been mistaken.

"As I told you over the telephone, I'm not allowed to give out that information. Our guests expect a certain level of privacy here, and we are determined to provide it."

It was time to try a new tack. I took a twenty from my wallet and slid it across the desk. "Perhaps you could look again."

If he saw the bill, he ignored it, though I noticed that a maid ten feet away was watching the attempted bribe with unconcealed mirth in her gaze. She was an older woman with a weathered face deeply lined from a thousand smiles and ten thousand tears. At least I'd made somebody happy tonight. That was something.

The desk clerk finally noticed the bill, and nearly sneered at it as he dismissed its presence. "Again, I'm sorry. I really can't help you."

I didn't know if he actually had integrity, or if he was holding out for more squeeze, but either way, we were finished. I couldn't afford any more on a lark, and he wasn't in the mood to share for free.

"Thanks, anyway," I said with as much mock sincerity as I could muster.

"You're most welcome," he replied, either not catching or ignoring my sarcasm completely.

I was at the Miata wondering what to do next when I saw the same maid who'd been watching us step outside, apparently for a smoking break. I didn't pay her much more attention, and then I saw her beckoning to me. What did I have to lose? I got out of the car and walked toward her.

"Can I help you?" I asked.

"No, but I can help you. I understand you're looking for somebody."

I nodded. "I am, but your clerk in there wasn't very cooperative."

She laughed, then said, "Don't mind Jeffrey. He got caught stealing supplies from the office last week, and it's just your bad luck the man's on probation. It must have broken his heart to pass up that twenty." She added with a wink, "I'm not on probation, though."

I dove into my pocket for the bill, and handed it to her. "Is Barry Hill staying here?"

"He is," she admitted. "He's in the Azalea Room, but he's not there right now."

"How do you know that?"

"I saw him out by the pool taking a smoke not two minutes before you walked in. Was that worth your twenty?"

"Every dime of it," I said as I hurried to the pool area. I stopped a second, then asked, "Can I borrow a cigarette?"

"Are you telling me a man driving a car like that can't afford his own smokes?"

"I could if I wanted them, but I need one as a prop. How else am I going to get him to talk to me?"

"Smart thinking," she said as she handed me a cigarette. "Take my advice. Shallow puffs, and try not to inhale or you'll choke to death on it."

I took the cigarette and walked to the pool. I wasn't a big fan of smoking, and it killed me that my home state of North Carolina made so much from the addictive habit, but I didn't have time to moralize. I needed this man to open up to me, and if holding a Winston could help, I'd do it.

I found a gentleman sitting by himself, the glowing ember of his lit cigarette intensifying as he took a drag from it.

"Mind if I join you?" I asked, holding the cigarette up.

"Be my guest," he said. "To be honest with you, I'd like the company."

I held the Winston long enough for him to see it, but I couldn't bring myself to light it, no matter what the stakes. Instinctively, I snapped it in half. Now what was I going to say?

I didn't have to come up with anything. He did it for me. "Trying to quit? I must have thrown away a hundred packs over the last six months, but I can't seem to make it stick."

"It's tough, isn't it?"

He stared at the cigarette in his hand, started to snuff it out, then took another drag. "It's the hardest thing I ever tried to do. I'll beat it one day, but for now, it helps me get through the night."

I sat on a chair nearby. "It sounds like you've got a heavy load on you."

He started to say something, then it looked as though he changed his mind. "We've all got our problems," he said.

"I've been told I'm a good listener," I said, "and I don't mind hearing what you've got to say."

He nodded in the near darkness. "It's a story that's been told a million times. I lost someone I thought I loved, and it's tearing me up inside."

"What happened?" I prodded when he didn't speak again. "Did it just happen?"

"In a way it did, but in other ways, I realize that I lost her a long time ago. I just didn't know it at the time."

"That sounds tough," I said. "How did you lose her?"

"That's exactly what I asked her this morning," he said softly. "You know the worst part about it? I'm not even sure I ever had her in the first place." He stared toward the pool, then added, "She was a cruel woman, and I'm sitting here in the dark wondering how I ever made myself believe she loved me." He lit a fresh cigarette off the dying butt in his fingertips, took a deep breath of it, then said with a jab of anger in his voice, "Who am I kidding? Why am I sitting around here mourning for her? I'm starting to think that maybe she got exactly what she deserved."

He stood up abruptly, flicked his cigarette toward the pool, then walked off without another word.

I sat there a second, then dialed Molly's number on my cell phone.

"Hey, it's Ben."

"I thought we were finished tonight, Ben. I'm busy."

"This is important," I said as I stood up and started back

to my Miata. "I thought you'd like to know that Connie Brown's former fiancé is staying out at the Lakefront Inn."

She lowered her voice as she said, "Ben, are you drunk? I'm looking at Brian Ross, and he's sitting twenty feet from me."

"Not that fiancé," I said. "I'm talking about the last one she dumped, Barry Hill."

"How did you find him?" she asked.

"I figured if he was hanging around Harper's Landing, he'd probably be at the Lakefront."

"And they just told you he was a guest?" she asked. "I know better than that. They treat that place like a fortress."

"Listen, do you want to sit here and argue about it over the telephone, or do you want to talk to the man? He's in the Azalea Room, but I'm not sure how long he's going to be here. I just talked to him, and it looked like he made up his mind about something."

"You're interrogating suspects now?" she asked loudly. "Now I'm hoping you're drunk and not just stupid."

"Don't let him get away," I said, ignoring the insult, and then I hung up.

I got into the Miata and started to take off, but then I realized that if Barry Hill did decide to flee, maybe I could follow him. I had a little practice tailing people, but I preferred my mother's minivan over my Miata. It was certainly less conspicuous.

I sat there for fifteen minutes, afraid Molly was going to disregard my plea, when I saw a cruiser pull up beside me.

Molly got out, and I joined her. "Why are you still here?" she asked.

"I wanted to make sure he didn't get away before you got here," I said.

"You're just a bucket of surprises today, aren't you?"

"Can I go with you when you talk to him?" I asked. "You might need a witness."

"Go home, Ben. I mean it."

I knew that tone of voice well enough to realize that she wasn't kidding. I got into the Miata, but before I drove off, I said, "Be careful. He could be a killer."

She nodded, then headed toward the inn.

I wanted to stay and wait, not just to find out what Molly uncovered, but more importantly, to make sure she was safe. I'd never be able to live with myself if something happened to her because of me, and I knew Molly wouldn't be in danger right now if I hadn't interfered with police business. Maybe *interfere* was too strong a word. *Circumnavigate* was probably more appropriate.

I chided myself to stop stalling. Molly had been clear enough about her desire for me to leave. I knew if I stayed and disregarded her direct order, our relationship would be seriously damaged, maybe permanently.

Still, driving off and leaving her all alone with a man who might be a murderer was one of the hardest things I'd ever had to do in my life. I couldn't bring myself to drive home, so instead, I wandered around in my car, not sure where to go. When an hour passed and I still hadn't heard from Molly, I decided to drive back to the Lakefront, despite her earlier warning.

Her squad car was gone.

I dialed her number on my cell phone, and of course it was busy. When I finally got through to her, I said, "Where have you been? Why didn't you call me?"

"Sorry, Mom," Molly said. "I didn't mean to miss my curfew. Don't ground me, please. I really want to go to the spring dance."

"How did it go?" I asked, ignoring the sarcasm.

"He was packing his things," she said. "I managed to persuade him to hang around town a little while, and he wasn't too happy about it."

"So you think he might have killed her?" I asked.

"I'm not ruling anybody out right now," Molly said. "I've got to go, Ben. I'm working late tonight."

And then she hung up on me, without a thank you or any indication that I'd helped her in her investigation. I wasn't doing it for her gratitude, but I wouldn't have minded a little acknowledgment that I'd actually been of some use. Then I realized that if Molly had thanked me, she would have tacitly been admitting that she'd needed me, and that wasn't about to happen.

I was going to have to be content that I'd managed to get some of the intense glare of the police's focus off of Diana. And after all, that was exactly what I was trying to do.

It was time to shake another branch of this tree and see what came falling out.

I tried to track Betsy Blair down the same way I'd found Barry Hill, but I didn't have any luck. After I'd visited all of the nearby motels in the area, I decided to give up and go back home. There was a call on my answering machine from Diana, asking me to call her, no matter how late I got in.

"Hey, it's me," I said when she picked up.

"I owe you an apology," she said.

"Did something happen that I missed?"

"You know what I'm talking about. I ran you off this evening, and all you wanted to do was help. What did you end up eating for dinner?"

I didn't want to admit that I'd dined with Molly, but

I knew Diana would find out tomorrow, given that the folks in Harper's Landing didn't have a whole lot to talk about other than each other. "Molly and I grabbed something at The Hound Dog."

"How nice for you both," she said with a tone that shouted *you'd better start explaining yourself, and fast.*

"It was business, actually," I added. "I wanted to share my suspicions with her, and see if she'd let any information slip out about the case."

"How did she take your meddling?"

"Better than I had any right to expect, actually. She seemed interested when I told her about my conversation with Sharon, the contessa's assistant."

"When did you have time to talk to her? Or did you take her out, too?"

"We did take a walk around town," I said, realizing that Diana would probably hear about that, too. My life was getting more complicated than I liked.

Diana sighed, then said, "Well, at least you weren't with Kelly."

"She called me this evening, and I went by her office before I came to see you."

There was a moment's hesitation, and I held my breath as I waited for her reaction. The laugh I got wasn't expected at all.

"What's so funny?"

She caught her breath and said, "You're a pretty popular fellow with the ladies lately, aren't you?"

"You'd think so, but I didn't have much luck with any of them, including the only one who is supposed to still be my girlfriend. Well, that's not entirely true, either."

"Which part?"

I rubbed my face with my free hand. "Can we start this conversation over?"

"Not on your life," she said, and I swear I could hear in her voice that she was smiling. "This is just starting to get good."

"I give up, then," I said. "Would you like to hear my conclusions so far?"

"Why not? Just one thing, though."

"What's that?"

"I don't want to hear my name on your list of suspects."

"Believe me," I said, "that might be one of Molly's theories, but it's not one of mine."

"And don't list my aunt and uncle, either. They are no more capable of murder than I am."

I took a deep breath, then said, "You know, I didn't even think about them. They certainly had a reason to want Connie Brown dead, didn't they?"

"Ben, that's not even funny. There's no way that Aunt Amy or Uncle Paul would ever harm anyone."

"Diana, I'm not saying they could. I just don't want to see you go to jail because the police were too stubborn to look at anybody else."

She paused, then asked softly, "You know something? You never even asked me if I did it."

"I've been working on the assumption that you were innocent," I agreed. "Shouldn't I have?"

The next thing I knew, she hung up on me. Okay, maybe it had been a little out of line. I sat there staring at the phone for a minute, wondering what I should do, when it rang.

"I'm so glad you called back," I said before even waiting for a comment. "I didn't mean anything by it. I swear I didn't."

Instead of Diana's voice, Molly chuckled and asked, "What did you do this time? Never mind, I don't want to know. Listen, have you seen Jeff?"

"Is this a cop asking, or my brother's girlfriend?"

"Guess," she said. "So have you seen him?"

"No, but you might try the shop. Use the private line." We had a line for family and friends that wasn't published anywhere. Though it was an added expense to our bottom line, none of us cared.

"I did, but no one picked up."

"You might want to try Jim, then," I said. "Sometimes they hang out together after work."

"Thanks. Bye."

Before I could ask a question myself, Molly hung up.

The phone rang again before I could put it back down. "That took longer to get through than I thought it would," Diana said.

"Molly just called," I explained.

"My, you are popular, aren't you?"

"She was looking for my brother. Listen, I didn't mean that last bit like it sounded."

"Do you mean that Molly didn't call for Jeff?"

"Diana, don't make this harder on me than it has to be. You know exactly what I mean."

She sighed, then said, "Of course I do. I just thought that you'd believe in me without any explanation necessary."

"I never doubted you," I said firmly.

"That wasn't how it sounded to me."

"That's what I meant."

"Good, I'm glad we got that cleared up. Good night."

And then she hung up on me again, this time before I could wish her a good night myself. I knew she had reason enough to be sensitive, but I wasn't about to apologize for something I didn't do. I turned off the ringer and set the answering machine volume to zero. I needed some rest, and the way my night was going, I wasn't going to get any if I didn't take steps to protect my space. Anybody who really needed me knew where I lived. Let them bang on my front door if it's an emergency, but otherwise, I wanted the world to leave me alone, at least for tonight.

THE next morning, I checked my answering machine after I dragged myself out of bed. There were no messages, and I wasn't sure if I should feel good about that or not. Maybe I wasn't all that important after all. Before I forgot, I turned the ringer back on just as it jumped to life.

It was my sister Louisa.

"Can you talk?" she asked.

"Of course I can. What makes you ask that?"

"I tried calling you earlier, and you didn't pick up. When I heard your answering machine kick in, I thought you might have an overnight guest."

"No, I've been here by myself all night. What's up?"

"You need to come in to the shop early this morning," she said. "The rest of us are already here."

"What on earth is going on now?"

"Nobody died or anything," Louisa said with her normal bluntness. "Kate's going to demonstrate how to make lip balm and hand lotion to all of us."

"I could probably live with missing that," I said.

"Could you survive being AWOL at a family meeting?" she asked. "Mom called this gathering, not Kate. For some reason, she's really pushing this expansion. If I didn't know better, I'd say our dear sweet mother was behind it herself."

"Why would she do that?" I asked. Family was family, but business was business. Mom tried her best never to let her personal feelings affect the decisions she made, but I knew how impossible that was for her sometimes.

"I can't say," Louisa said, an odd choice of words for my sister. Her voice had suddenly become guarded.

"Because you don't know, or you're not allowed to tell?"

She hesitated far longer than she should have. "It's the second one."

"Louisa, are you holding out on me? What's going on?"

"Just come and see for yourself," she said.

"Is Mom standing right there?"

"Yes, that's true."

That explained the sudden change in her demeanor. "Okay, that's fair enough. I'll be there soon, and we'll talk about it then."

She paused, then said, "No, I don't think so. It doesn't look like rain at all. Bye."

Louisa certainly knew how to get my curiosity stoked. What was the secret she knew, and more importantly, why hadn't anyone else told me? I hadn't had any luck getting her to tell me over the telephone, but if I could pressure her in person, she might just crack, especially since it was pretty obvious to me that she was dying to tell me anyway. I took a shower and dressed in record time, and less than half an hour later I was walking into Where There's Soap.

"Sorry I'm late," I said as I saw my family gathered around Kate in the classroom. "I didn't get the memo in time."

"If you'd answer your telephone, Benjamin, you might know what's going on with your family. What's wrong with that answering machine of yours? I tried to leave a message, but it never came on."

"I must have hit the off button instead of the volume control," I admitted. "Sorry about that."

"Just take a seat," she said. "We don't have a great deal of time."

Kate said, "Mom, this can wait. There's nothing urgent about getting started now that I've got the approval."

"Kate, that's exactly the wrong approach here," Mom said. "I want to get going with this new line now that we've all agreed, and we can't sell something we don't know how to make. We are your students, and class is in session. Benjamin, take a seat."

I took a stool beside Louisa. "What's going on? Why the big push here?"

She wanted to answer, I could see it in her eyes, but then Mom said, "We don't have much time, so let's dispense with the chatting, shall we?" She stared right at me as she said it, and I finally nodded, as much to get her focus off me as anything else.

Kate had supplies laid out up front at the teaching table. "To start with, we're going to use kits to make the process easier to grasp. Jeff, would you hand these out?"

My youngest brother retrieved four kits and passed them out. As he did, Kate said, "We'll be working in teams, since these things aren't cheap."

Louisa and I were partnered, and I started tearing the cellophane off our kit.

"Don't wait for me. Go ahead and open them," Kate said, grinning at me.

"Sorry I jumped the gun," I said as I started spreading the contents out on the worktable. I was more used to being in the front of the classroom instead of at one of the students' tables, but it was good to take a class every now and then, not just to learn something new, but to see the room from a different perspective.

The kit had labeled containers of dyes, fragrances, lotion bases, and beeswax beads. There were also several different kinds of receptacles to hold the products we were making, along with fancy blank labels, and a few odd-looking eyedroppers thrown in as well.

"As you can see," Kate said, "many of the things we already use for soapmaking are in the kit. That's why I think this is a perfect match." She studied her notes a second, then said, "We're going to start with lotion, since it's the easiest to do. I don't want to rush you boys too fast."

Bob said, "Stick to teaching and leave the editorials to someone else."

"Mom," Kate said, "you told them to cooperate."

She shot Bob a quick look, then said to Kate, "He's right. Go on, and try to do it without the sidebars."

Kate didn't look the least bit chastised by the comment. She addressed us, saying, "After you put the dispensing cap on the big bottle of shea butter, squeeze enough into one of the lotion bottles until it's halfway full."

Jeff asked, "Which bottle is for the lotion?"

Cindy, his partner and our youngest sibling, shook an odd-sized container in front of him. "This is what you want." She held up a small tube and said, "This is for lip balm, and so is this," she added as she held up a small transparent plastic canister.

"Come on, get with the program," I said to Jeff, though in all honesty, I hadn't been 100 percent positive myself.

"Sorry," he said. "I'm not in touch with my feminine side like you are."

I started to retort, but a swift slap on the top of the head brought Jeff back in line more than anything I could say. Hitting wasn't allowed in our family, unless the blow came from Mom.

Kate went on. "Go ahead, everybody fill up a lotion container, but remember, just do it half full."

We did as we were told. At least most of us did. As simple as it was, Bob was having trouble. "Hey, the lid won't fit."

Mom, who was Bob's partner by default, took the small lid from him and gave him the capped one. Then she said, "This one was from the bottle, remember?"

I started to laugh, tried to kill it, and ended up choking. "Ben, are you all right?" Louisa asked.

"I'm fine," I said, getting it back under control again. I was beginning to realize our family's division of labor was sound and well thought out. When it came to big equipment, my brothers were masters, but if something needed to be done on an individual basis, many times they were lost. I felt fortunate to be able to float between production and our customers, never mastering either one entirely, but being able to function nonetheless.

Kate held up a small bottle and said, "Now add dye to your container. We've got seafoam green and luscious lavender, so take your pick. Remember, it's potent, so a few drops are probably all you need."

I chose the green, added a few drops, then snuck a few more in.

Kate continued. "Put the lid back on, then shake it up. After you have it mixed, put in more lotion until there's just a little room at the top. Shake it up again, and it's ready to use."

"That's it?" Louisa asked, clearly disappointed.

"That's the basic process, but here's something cool you

can do." She approached our table with a clean bottle of
her own. While I'd chosen green, Louisa had gone with the
lavender. Kate squeezed half of my bottle into hers, then
topped it off with Louisa's. It was a neat trick, since the
colors stayed separate. "There's lots you can do, but that
will have to wait. Now let's move on to lip balms."

"Hey, I want to do a layered one, too," Jeff said.

"Now who's got the feminine side," I said.

"It's for Molly," he added, then ducked Mom's strike
from behind. "That's not fair. I'm trying to learn how to do
this."

Mom relented. "Surely we have a moment to spare," she
said to Kate.

"Absolutely. Go ahead, we've got plenty of empty bottles. Just remember, after you use half, add more dye, then
top it off again with shea butter."

Once we had our mixes, Kate said, "Now, let's move on.
Take your beeswax beads and put them in the microwav-
able glass bowls I handed out. Add the sunflower oil, then
nuke the contents at high power for thirty seconds. Stir
your mixture and keep going until the wax is melted. It
should take about two minutes."

"Why not go for two minutes straight then?" I asked.

"Stirring helps it all get incorporated," Kate said. After
we did as we were told, we pulled our bowls out. "Now add
color and flavor if you'd like it. We're not going to split
these like we did the lotion, but you can mix and layer lip
balms, too. Be careful, the mixture's hot. When you've got
what you want, pipe it into the tubes or canisters and let
them cool. Oh, one thing. Give the tubes a few minutes,
then add another few drops to make up for air bubbles and
settling."

We all worked together, chatting as we went. The mix

was hot; I could attest to that when some accidentally sloshed out on me. After two minutes, Louisa tried to pipe more balm into the top of her tube. "It's already set up."

Kate nodded. "Just microwave it for another thirty seconds, then you'll be ready to go again. Your pipette is going to be full, too, so just squeeze it out like you would a tube of toothpaste, and you're ready to go again."

I hadn't been all that excited to learn how to make lip balm and hand lotion, and I hadn't been afraid to admit it, but the results had turned out pretty cool, and if Diana was still speaking to me, I'd have a few thoughtful little gifts to help smooth things over between us.

I was feeling pretty good about my creations when my cell phone rang.

"Are we finished, Kate?" I asked.

"We are. Thank you all."

I let the phone ring, then started applauding. My family soon followed, and our clapping filled the classroom. Sometime in the applause, the ringing had stopped.

Kate took it all in, then Mom said, "It's time to open. Ben, after you take that call, help your sister clean up."

"Which sister?" Louisa asked.

"I think Kate should do it, since it was her class," Cindy added.

Mom was about to rule when Kate said, "I don't mind, really. It was fun."

"You've been reprieved," Mom said to Louisa and Cindy. That's when I noticed that my brothers were already gone. It appeared that they'd made their escape as soon as I'd drawn the assignment to help. I'd find a way to get them back. After all, what were big brothers for?

Kate and Mom started to clean up, and I checked my phone to see who had called. It was a number I didn't recognize, so I dialed it and was surprised when a woman answered.

"I understand you've been looking for me," she said.

It took me a second to realize who it was. "Is this Betsy Blair?"

"How many other women have you been hunting down like dogs? I don't appreciate the effort, Mr. Perkins."

I nearly asked her how she'd gotten my number when I realized that one of the hotel clerks I'd left it with must have passed it on to her after denying she was staying there. If I ever had a tryst, I'd do it there. I hadn't had a clue one of them had lied to me.

"I don't have all day," she said. "I'm checking out in one hour, so if you want to talk to me, you'll have to get out here by then."

"I would, if I knew where you were staying," I said.

Her laugh was like a hyena's bark. "Good point. I'm at the Mountain Lake. Are you familiar with it?"

"I've been there a time or two," I said, trying to decide if I was going to tell Molly about my rendezvous.

"I'll just bet you have," she said, then added another wicked laugh. "I'm in room thirteen. There's just one thing, though. No cops, do you understand me? I'll talk to you, but if anyone else shows up, I'm going to get a case of amnesia that will make your head fall off. Understand?"

I could always catch Molly up later if I learned anything. "I understand. I'll be right there."

I made my excuses, then tore out of the soap shop toward the motel. Maybe I was finally going to get some answers.

SEVEN

∘ ∘ ∘

THE door to room thirteen was standing wide open, and for a second I thought Betsy had left without waiting for me. Then I had an eerie premonition as I stepped inside. For the oddest reason, the hair on the back of my neck stood at attention, and I had an overwhelming feeling in my gut that she was dead.

"You must be Ben Perkins," an overweight woman with brassy highlights said as she came out of the bathroom. So much for my second sight.

She had a makeup bag in her hands, but I was surprised there was any left after seeing the heavy application on her face. She must have bought it by the barrel, the way she'd so lavishly applied it.

"I am," I admitted. "I'm curious about something, Betsy. Why did you agree to see me?"

She put the makeup bag in her suitcase. "You just named it yourself. Curiosity killed more than the cat, didn't it? I thought to myself, now why in the world would a soapmaker by trade want to talk to me? Are you looking for tips, perhaps?"

"I appreciate the offer, but I'm a decent craftsman myself. No, I'm here to talk to you about your lawsuit."

"How disappointing," she said. "And I was hoping we could trade some secrets about our profession."

"Are you a professional soapmaker, too?" I asked.

"I don't have that pleasure, thanks to Connie Brown. I absolutely refuse to call her *the contessa*. She stole my book, and my best chance at ever being recognized as a talent in the industry."

"It sounds like you really hated her," I said as I leaned against the door frame.

She laughed, then said, "Don't try your tricks on me, Ben. I won't be goaded into a confession. Think about it. Why would I want her dead? Now that she's out of the picture, it will be impossible to prove to the world that her last book—the one that everyone on earth says was her best book—was really mine. No, I'm afraid the hunt for my satisfaction died with her. I'm giving up."

"There's still her estate," I said.

"I won't sue a dead woman," Betsy said fiercely, then quickly regained her composure. "I hope you find the killer. They deprived me of my dream, and I hope they pay for it."

"I thought your dream was to be published?" I asked. Betsy Blair's words were rational enough, but there was an undertone in her voice that made me wonder if the woman was quite mad.

"That would have been the icing, but the cake would have been to see the great contessa exposed as the thief she was. And now I've been robbed of even that." She latched her suitcase, then hefted it. "How dreary of you to seek me out just to ask me such mundane questions. It's too bad you didn't want any tips from me. In all modesty, I'm very good."

"I'm sure you are," I said.

"You don't believe me, do you?" She dug into her suitcase and came up with a bound manuscript. "Read it and see if I don't know what I'm talking about. I had this made up for the trial, so feel free to keep it."

I took it from her, then on a whim, I handed it back to her and asked, "Would you mind signing it for me?" I figured if I stroked her ego a little, maybe I'd get something useful out of her.

She looked startled by the very idea of it, and as she rummaged around in her purse for a pen, I could swear she was blushing. She signed the top page with a flowery scrawl, then handed it back to me. "Thank you," she said softly.

"Thank you," I said. "So, what's next for you?"

"I'm going to write another book. This time, though, I'm not showing it to anyone but a reputable publisher. I did it once. I'm going to prove I can do it again."

As she started to go, I asked, "By the way, where were you yesterday afternoon?"

Betsy waved a finger in the air toward me. "Don't be tedious, Ben. Do you really want the last thing you say to me to be a request for an alibi?"

"You can't blame me for being curious," I said.

"No," she said with a smile. "I suppose not." She shut the door behind us, then put her bag in the back of a banged-up old Saturn. I thought she was going to just drive off, but before she did, she said, "I'm not the one you should be asking for an alibi."

"Who else did you have in mind?"

"Someone who was about to be fired."

"Are you talking about Sharon?"

"Ask her yourself," Betsy said.

"Why don't you come with me? After all, you're the one who eavesdropped on their conversation."

She didn't deny it. "And what on earth could possibly be in it for me? That's what makes the world wag its tail, Ben, never forget it."

Before I could answer, she drove away. As I wrote her license plate number down on the palm of my hand, I could still hear her laughing.

I called Molly, who answered grumpily, "What?"

"I just talked to Betsy Blair, and she had an interesting take on Connie Brown's murder you should hear."

"Ben, don't start with me. I've had a bad morning, and it just keeps getting worse."

"Don't you at least want to hear what she had to say?"

There was a short pause, then Molly said, "Go ahead, but make it dance."

I think "Betsy eavesdropped on Connie's room while she was staying in town, and she heard Connie fighting with Sharon. She claims the contessa fired her assistant just before she was murdered."

I could hear Molly sigh loudly. "I can't use any of that: it is nothing but hearsay, and if you weren't such an amateur, you would know it, too."

"At least talk to her," I said.

"Don't you think I have? Ben, stick to your soapmaking and leave the detecting to me."

And then she hung up on me.

I was too angry to drive, so I sat there until I could calm myself down. Molly knew just how to tweak my pride, and

I wish I could get over the jabs she took at me, but unfortunately, I hadn't figured out a way to do that yet. On a whim, I picked up the manuscript Betsy had signed for me and leafed through it. It wasn't half bad, actually. Her points were lucid and well thought out, and I found myself easily following her steps and procedures. From teaching classes myself, I knew that wasn't as easy as it looked. Something caught my eye as I scanned the document, and I realized that one of the techniques she was suggesting was more than a little familiar. Where had I seen it, though? Then I realized that it had come from Connie's new book, with little effort made to hide its source. But the real question was still which document had come first.

I hated to admit it, but I wasn't getting anywhere in my investigation. I thought of a dozen things I could do, but what I ended up deciding on was going back to the shop. It seemed that every time I tried to help, I kept getting smacked in the nose for my trouble. If it weren't for Diana's involvement with the murder victim—and the fact that our back room was the murder scene—I'd turn my back on the whole thing without a single look over my shoulder.

I was involved in it, though, whether I liked it or not.

As I drove, I realized that I couldn't let Molly brush me off like that. I had given her pertinent information—at least I thought it was important—and she was going to take it seriously.

I took a chance and went by her office, but she wasn't there, and the man behind the desk wouldn't tell me where she was. I had an idea, though. It was approaching lunchtime, and I knew she and my brother liked to eat together whenever they could. All I had to do was go back to Where There's Soap and hope she showed up.

Sometimes it's better to be lucky than good. At least that's what I thought as I pulled into the back parking lot of Where There's Soap and saw Molly's squad car parked there. She was sitting in the driver's seat talking on the radio as I approached her, and I could hear her say, "It's okay, George, you did the right thing. No, it's fine. He's standing right here. I don't need backup to handle him, trust me."

She got out of the squad car. "You've got to stop showing up at my office. Half the force believes you're stalking me, and the other half thinks you're pining away for my long lost love."

"You wish," I said, without hesitation.

I'd been flip about it, but apparently she wasn't in the mood. "No, actually, I'd hoped you'd get bored and find a new hobby. I'm tired of having you nipping at my heels all of the time."

"Hey, that's not fair. Sometimes I get there before you do," I said, letting my voice's intensity match hers.

"Ben, when are you going to get it through your head that I don't need your help? I'm a good cop. Why can't you believe that?"

"I do," I said. "Molly, I'm not trying to make you look bad when I dig into these things. But I wish you'd at least acknowledge that sometimes I manage to come up with something you've missed."

"Let's see, you just insulted my work ethic, my professional competence, and my honor. How on earth could any of that make me mad?"

"I'm not trying to charm you," I said. "I had some valuable information to share with you, but because of your stubborn pride, she's probably long gone."

Molly looked at me and frowned. "Are you still talking

about Betsy Blair? I can't listen to whatever she told you. It won't stand up in court."

"Then go talk to her yourself. She checked out of the Mountain Lake Motel, but I've got her license plate number. Find her and talk to her."

"What's the plate number?" she asked as she got back into her car and turned the radio up.

I held my palm up where I'd written it.

She stared at it a second, then asked, "Do you honestly expect me to do anything with this?"

I looked at my hand and saw that the number was smudged beyond recognition. "It started with a *J.* I'm pretty sure of that."

"Sorry, but it's not enough." She turned her radio back off and got out.

"Aren't you going to at least talk to her?" I asked.

"You told me she was gone, remember? What do you expect me to do about it?"

Before I could say anything else, Jeff came out on the back steps. "I could hear you two fighting all the way inside. What's going on?"

I looked at him and said, "We're not fighting. We're just having a difference of opinion."

He looked at Molly, who wouldn't make eye contact. "That's what I thought. Ben, if you'll excuse us, we're late for our lunch."

"We're not finished here," I said.

Molly shook her head. "I'm sorry, but we are. Bye, Ben."

She and Jeff walked to his car, and he held the door open for her. After they were gone, I walked inside the soap shop. Why wouldn't Molly listen to me? I could help her, if only she weren't so stubborn.

"You look like you just lost your best friend," my youngest sister Cindy said as I walked into the boutique area of our business.

"The funny thing is, I think I just might have."

The look of sympathy on her face was undeniable. "Ben, I'm so sorry. Would you like to talk about it?"

I studied my sister and saw the concern on her face. I bit back my first reaction of serving up a sarcastic remark and patted her hand. "I appreciate the offer, but I just want to forget it ever happened."

"Fine, but if you want to talk, I'm always here for you."

I smiled at her. "Cindy, I'm supposed to be the wiser, older sibling here. I should be offering comfort instead of getting it."

She offered me one of her perfect grins. "I don't happen to need any at the moment, but when I do, you'll be the first one I call. If you're sure you don't need me, I'm taking off for a long lunch. I've got a big date."

"Anybody I know?" I asked.

"Oh, no you don't. If Louisa, Kate, and Mom can't get it out of me, I'm certainly not going to tell you. For now, just think of him as a mystery man."

"I'd like to meet him before you two go out," I said. Since Dad had died, I'd taken over the role of keeping tabs on my siblings, and screening my sisters' dates was high on that list.

"I'm sure you would," she said, and then she escaped while she could.

I found Kate and Louisa stocking the new lotion and balm section. "That didn't take long," I said.

"Mom insisted," Kate said. "And as long as she's willing to let me try it, I'm not going to get in the way. What do you think about what we've got so far?"

I studied the layout. They'd filled half the space with craft kits on lotions and balms, and the other shelves were full of supplies. "It's fine," I said.

Kate wasn't about to let me get away with that. "Come on, give. What's wrong with it?"

"Do you really want my opinion?" I asked.

"Would I have asked for it if I didn't? I'm not saying I'll do what you say, but I do want to hear your thoughts."

I looked at Louisa. "How about you?"

"Don't drag me into this. I'm just her helper. She's making all of the executive decisions."

I nodded. "Okay, here's what I think you should do. Take all that clutter off the top shelf and make an instructional display on how easy the products are to make. You're clever, use your imagination."

"But if the shelf doesn't have any products on it, how are we going to make money off it?"

I knew Mom drilled everyone in our business on making every square inch of the store count, so it wasn't an unreasonable question. "Kate, they need to see the steps if you're going to sell many kits. Once you get them hooked on the process, then you'll get repeat sales. Trust me, though, I'd demo it first."

Kate nodded. "I'll think about it." She turned to Louisa and asked, "What do you think?"

"I think whatever you decide will be perfect."

"Come on," Kate said to her. "Don't be afraid to slam Ben's idea just because he's standing right here with us."

Louisa laughed. "As if I would. Honestly, you'll get some flak from Mom, but I think the idea makes sense." She patted me on the arm. "Wow, I knew you'd have to be right sooner or later. After all, you can't blatantly keep ignoring the law of averages your entire life."

"Thanks for the boost," I said.

"Hey, that's why I'm here."

As Kate worked on the how-to display, I helped Louisa with the sales floor. We hadn't scheduled any classes for the week, thinking we wouldn't have the time or the energy after our Soap Celebration. It was just one more area where our bottom line would take a hit.

I worked with my sisters as they took turns going to lunch. I wasn't that hungry, and it felt good waiting on customers instead of chasing down dead end after dead end. It seemed that everywhere I turned there were too many suspects, but no way of proving any of them had been directly involved in Connie Brown's murder.

"Ben, you need to take lunch. It's nearly three o'clock," Cindy said as Kate got back. "We never expected you to work here all afternoon."

"That's true," Louisa said. "You've earned a lunch break."

"I'm fine," I insisted.

Kate looked at me and said, "We're sure you have other things to do."

"Are you all trying to get rid of me?"

Louisa grinned. "Give the man a cigar. Seriously, we have a routine, and you're stepping all over it. It's nice to have you fill in, but we can handle it from here on out."

"I don't know when I've ever been so insulted in my life," I said, trying to hide my grin.

"Come on, it can't be that hard to figure out," Louisa said. "How about the time—"

I cut her off before she could finish. "Thanks, but I don't need a recap of Ben's snubs. I get the hint. I'm going."

The three of them collapsed on me, putting me in the

direct center of a group hug. "You know we love you," Kate said.

"Though we're not sure why," Louisa added.

Cindy said, "Don't pay any attention to them. You know you're the best big brother a girl could ask for."

"You'd better be careful saying that," I told Cindy. "You've got four big brothers."

"You know what I mean," she said.

I made my way out of the crowd, and Kate asked, "Do you feel better now?"

"As rejections go, that was pretty nice," I admitted. "Now I'm going to get out of here before you change your minds."

"You don't have to worry about that," Louisa said.

I took off. As my stomach started to rumble, I decided I could eat a bite or two after all. The only thing was, I didn't want to eat alone. I thought about calling Diana, but then decided I'd go ahead and drop by her bookstore just in case she could get away. I hadn't had a chance to spend any time with her since the murder, and I needed her as my touchstone.

Dying To Read was crowded with customers, but Rufus was ignoring them. Instead, he had a series of photographs laid out on the sales counter, and he was peering at different shots with a photographer's loupe.

"Is your boss around?"

He looked up at me and grinned. "I have no superior, but if you want Diana, she's hiding back in her office."

"Is it that bad?" I asked softly. Diana was an extrovert who had a true love for her mystery readers. That's when I realized that they must have all been there to experience a real murder vicariously. Instead of killing her business as a suspect, Diana was probably more popular selling books than she ever had been before.

Rufus's head bobbed. "It's pretty tough. She hasn't even been to lunch yet. I don't think she's coming out."

"I'll take care of that," I said as I made my way to her office. I knocked once, waited, then knocked again. Could she have slipped out without Rufus realizing it? "Diana? It's Ben."

I heard movement, then the door opened slowly.

"Come in, but make it fast."

I slipped inside, and she clicked the lock in place behind me. "Are the vultures still out there?" she asked.

"If you mean your customers, there's a pretty good crowd assembling. Are you okay?"

She looked frazzled. Diana had pulled her dark hair back in a ponytail, but a great many errant strands had escaped. Her makeup was barely applied, and the bags under her eyes told me she hadn't gotten much sleep the night before.

"I've been better," she admitted.

"Let's get you out of here," I said. "This can't be doing you any good."

She shrugged. "I can't just bail out on Rufus. I know my customers mean well, but they've been driving me crazy with their theories on what really happened to Connie Brown. That's not the worst part of it, though. Some of them think I actually did it, and they're full of advice on how to fool the police. One man even lectured me on how to beat a polygraph test."

"Are you honestly doing Rufus any good staying back here behind a locked door?" I asked. "He asked me himself to get you out of here. The kid's unflappable. Instead of paying any attention to your customers, he's looking at his photographs."

"He's got the bug pretty bad," she said. "I just hope I don't lose him to the Camera Corner. Good help is tough to find on what I can pay."

"Do you honestly think anybody else is going to cut him the slack you do? I've got a feeling you're pretty safe. So what do you say? Do you want to break out of this joint?"

"They'll never let me out of here without a fight," she said. "But if you can come up with something, I'm game."

I thought about it a few seconds, then said, "Here's what we'll do. I'll create a diversion up front and you slip out the back. I'm parked down the street, and the Miata's unlocked. I'll see you there."

"Where are we going to go?" she asked. "I'm starving, but I can't take everybody staring at me. They've already convicted me in their minds. I can feel it every time somebody looks at me."

"We can grab a pizza to go, then take it back to my apartment. Or your place, if you'd prefer that."

"I don't care where we go. Let's just get out of here."

I nodded. "Give me a minute, and when you hear a commotion up front, run."

She touched my arm. "What are you going to do?"

"I'll figure that out once I'm up there." I kissed her lightly on the forehead. "See you soon."

I walked out of her office, and noticed that several people had been watching her door. Diana hadn't been paranoid. It appeared that many of the shoppers there really were trying to get a glimpse of her. I walked to the front window near Rufus and said in as loud a voice as I could, "Rufus, is that a body on the square?"

That got everyone's attention, including the store clerk's. "Where? I don't see a body."

"Keep your voice down and follow my lead," I said. In a louder voice, I added, "See? It's right there."

"You're right. Oh, man, I think that's blood," he said, the delight in his voice evident. That was all it took to get every patron of the store to the front window. I glanced back and saw Diana slip out the back way, then said, "No, it was just a shadow, but it looked real to me. Sorry."

There were more murmurs of disappointment than I ever would have imagined. From conversations with Diana in the past, I knew that mystery lovers fell into distinct categories, and I suspected most of the folks there at the moment were the hard-boiled types who enjoyed reading about violence. I loved traditional mysteries myself, preferring a book by Agatha Christie, Carolyn Hart, or Charlotte MacLeod any day. I liked it when the townspeople's characters were dissected more than the victim.

After Rufus and I were alone again, he asked softly, "What was that about?"

Before I could answer, he snapped his fingers. "It was a diversion, wasn't it? Diana's already out the back door, isn't she?"

I grinned and nodded. "It appeared to work, too."

Rufus buffed his fingernails on his shirt. "I was pretty convincing, wasn't I?"

If he wanted to delude himself into believing he'd known what I was up to, that was fine with me. "You fooled me, and I'm the one who set it up," I said. "See you later."

"Yeah," he said absently as he went back to his photographs.

Diana was sitting in the Miata waiting for me. As I got in, I said, "That went well, don't you think?"

"You and Rufus should take your act on the road," she

said. "I was so mesmerized I almost forgot your perfor-
mances were for my benefit."

"According to Rufus, he's the reason everyone believed
us." I drove toward my apartment, planning to stop off at a
pizza place on the way.

"Ben, could we pick up a few hamburgers instead? I'm
starving, and I don't know if I can wait for a pizza."

I agreed, and we grabbed a couple of burgers along the
way. "So where should we eat?"

"Let's go back to my place. I'd suggest a picnic, but I
just want to be alone."

I drove to her apartment, but there was a news van
parked in front, and we saw several people standing
around, obviously waiting for her.

"Keep driving," she said as she ducked down.

"I can't believe this," I said as I passed them. "They're
staking out your apartment."

"I should have warned you. They came by the bookstore
earlier, and Rufus told them I was at home."

After we were safely away, I said, "I can almost guaran-
tee you there won't be anybody waiting for you at my
place."

"Could we just eat right here? I'm starving."

"Why not? Should I put the top down?"

She thought about it, then reluctantly shook her head.
"We'd better not. I don't want anybody to spot us."

I nodded. "That's probably smart thinking." As she
handed out the food, we had a little picnic after all. Though
the Miata hadn't been designed for doing much but driving, we still managed to eat within the confines of the car.

"Every now and then I love indulging in fast food,"
Diana admitted.

"I'm shocked, shocked I tell you," I said with a grin.

"I know, it's my shameful secret. So what's yours?"

I hung my head down and pretended remorse. "It's too horrible to even speak," I said, trying to think of something I could admit.

"You can trust me with it," she said. "I'll take it to my grave."

"If you're sure it won't taint me forever in your eyes," I said.

"I promise I won't judge you."

"Well, I suppose you had to find out sooner or later." I paused, then confessed, "Sometimes, late at night when no one else is around, I watch infomercials. I don't mean to, but I'm flipping through the channels and I spot something, watch it a few seconds, then I'm hooked."

"That is bad," she admitted. "Have you ever ordered anything?"

"Just once, I swear it."

Diana nodded. "What did you buy?"

"I can't tell you. I'm too ashamed."

She touched my arm. "Ben, your secret is safe with me. Go on, tell me. You'll feel better about it."

"I got the greatest hits of the seventies," I said.

She couldn't keep a straight face any longer. "I've seen that commercial."

"Any time you want to listen to the complete catalog, just let me know."

"Thanks for the offer, but I think I'll pass."

I collected our trash, then asked, "So, where would you like to go now? If you can't face going back home, I'm sure one of my sisters would put you up until this blows over."

"Do you honestly think it's ever going to end? I can't

even blame them. If I didn't know I was innocent, I'd suspect myself, too. She killed my parents, Ben. How is that something I could ever forget, let alone forgive? You want to know something? If I'd known who she was, I actually might have done it."

I patted her hand. "But you didn't."

Diana started to cry, slowly at first, but then with more force. I tried my best to put my arm around her in the tight confines of the convertible, but I didn't have much luck.

"It's like losing them all over again," she whimpered. "It hurts so much."

"You shouldn't be alone," I said. "Come home with me."

"I can't." As she dried her tears, she said, "But I know where I need to be. Would you take me to my aunt and uncle's house?"

"I'd be happy to," I said. "You can stay as long as you'd like, and when you're ready to come back here, I'll be in their driveway waiting for you."

Her voice was deadly calm as she said, "I'm not sure when I'll be coming back. I can't take this scrutiny, it's driving me mad."

"You can take as much time as you need. I understand. How are you going to get your clothes?"

"I can't go back there," she said. "Don't worry, my aunt and I wear the same size. I'll borrow anything I need from her. Thanks for understanding."

"Hey, it's what I do best."

I drove her to Hunter's Hollow where they lived, but we paused outside in the driveway before she got out.

"At least let me walk you in," I said.

"It's better if we say good-bye right here." She leaned forward to give me a quick peck on the cheek, then popped out before I could get her door.

"Thanks, Ben. I'll call you."

"Tonight," I said.

"Tonight," she promised.

Her aunt and uncle must have been watching out the front door, because she was barely up the front steps when the door opened and they both came out. They wrapped her in their embrace, and Diana's uncle waved to me to show that everything was all right. I drove off, happy that Diana had somebody to turn to. It made me miss my father, but I was glad that I had such a large family around me. Most of the time relationships came and went, but family was always there. I didn't know how I could have survived without mine, and I was glad Diana had somewhere she could always go.

As I drove back to Harper's Landing, I wondered if Molly had interviewed Diana's aunt and uncle about the murder. After all, one of them had lost a sibling in that wreck, and if someone had killed one of my brothers or sisters—by accident or premeditation—I would have hunted them down myself.

I decided to stop off for a newspaper, since we were down to an afternoon edition of the local paper. I'd delivered the morning paper as a kid on my bicycle, passing the route down to any brother or sister who wanted it along the line. We'd had two healthy papers back then, but now we were down to one that was rumored to be failing. The talk around town was that they were going to have to come up with a big jump in revenues if they were going to make it.

When the headline screamed out at me as I paid for my paper, I realized they were going to try to drive their sales through the roof all at once, and at my family's expense.

EIGHT

● ● ●

"MURDER Revisits Local Business," the headline shouted.
There was a black-and-white photograph of Where There's
Soap just below the banner, and the photographer had
somehow managed to make the shop look evil and sinister,
as if the building itself had something to do with the homicides that had happened on our grounds. The story wasn't
much better. Whoever had written the article had dug up
every piece of dirt they could find about our business, and
after I read it, I wouldn't have wanted to shop there myself.
I bought four more papers, realizing that my family needed
to see this, and wouldn't be that patient in waiting to share.

My hands were shaking as I drove up to the shop. I'd
been gripping the steering wheel with a grasp that I wanted
to use on the reporter and editor who had so overtly
smeared us.

"Where's Mom?" I asked as I walked into a nearly deserted store. Had the article affected business already?

"I'm right here," she said, coming out from behind the register. "Benjamin, what's wrong?"

I slammed the papers down on the counter. "Have you seen this?"

She picked up the top copy, and soon every one of my brothers and sisters were reading it, some over the others' shoulders. By the time everyone had read it, we were ready to form a lynch mob.

Mom quelled us quickly enough. "Stop it," she said, silencing our protests. "That's enough."

"What are we going to do about this?" Louisa asked. "We can't let them get away with it."

"And what do you propose we do?" Mom asked calmly. "Is there anything they've printed here that's not true?"

"It's not what they said," Bob protested. "It's the way they said it. We should sue them."

"Newspapers slant stories from time to time. Is there a single one of you who's shocked by that? Of course not. I'm not any happier about this than you are, but we will weather this storm."

"Not unless we find out what really happened here," I said. "Until they have a killer to name, we're going to be their sensational headline."

She patted my shoulder. "Then it's more important than ever that you find the killer so Molly can arrest him."

"How do you suggest I do that?" I asked.

"Do what you're best at, Benjamin. Hit the hornet's nest with a stick and see what happens."

"What happens if I get stung?" I asked.

She frowned at me, then said, "You need to be careful so that doesn't happen."

"What are the rest of us supposed to do in the meantime?" Jim asked.

Mom clapped her hands together, her usual method of getting our attention. "Boys, you have enough orders to fill as it is. You've been complaining that you never manage to get caught up, so take advantage of this lull and do just that."

Kate said, "That's fine for them, but what about us?"

Mom waved a hand around the room. "There are lots of things we can do. I've been wanting to have a complete store inventory and cleaning, and what better time than when there aren't many customers here?"

Louisa asked, "You mean we have to count everything in here? It will take forever."

Mom clucked at her. "It's always a good time to do inventory. Trust me, children, there will be plenty of work for everyone. We have a nest egg held back for a rainy day, so no one's going to miss a paycheck."

Jim said, "I hope it's a monster of an egg. We're going to need it."

"Don't worry, we're going to be fine. Now let's all get busy, shall we? There's work to be done."

That seemed to satisfy them somewhat, so Mom pulled me away into the classroom. As soon as she shut the door, Mom said, "Benjamin, you must solve this quickly before we are ruined."

"What happened to the pep talk you just gave the rest of the family?" I asked.

"That was for the benefit of your brothers and sisters. This is serious. I won't have this family or this business ruined this way, and it's up to you to make sure neither happens. We can't allow them to drag our name through the mud. You must find the real killer, Benjamin."

"I'm trying," I said, "but it's hard."

"Of course it is," she said sympathetically. "That's why

it's your job. Is Diana distracting you from your work? Perhaps you should focus on this problem and spend less time with her. I approve of the dear girl, you know that, but we need your best."

"She's staying with family in Hunter's Hollow until this blows over," I admitted. "Seeing her too much won't be a problem."

Mom nodded. "That's the wisest thing to do. So, what are you going to do about this?"

I offered her a slight grin. "I'm going to go find a hornet's next and whack it with a stick."

"That's my boy," she said as she squeezed my cheek.

Now I just had to find the right nest to hit.

FROM everything I'd heard lately, I had to believe Sharon was still my most viable suspect, even if Molly didn't agree. It was time to talk to Connie Brown's assistant and see if there was a crack in her armor I could exploit.

I decided to walk to Jean Henshaw's bed-and-breakfast, since it was close to the soap shop. That had been one of the reasons I'd put the contessa there. I figured I'd be able to keep an eye on her if she was nearby. Man, oh man, had I been wrong.

It was a glorious day, but the sunshine and warm breeze were lost on me. I kept thinking about finding our guest speaker and star lying there on the floor of our shop. It was bad enough that someone had killed her, but why had they done it in Where There's Soap? Surely it would have been easier to strike when there wasn't a crowd of people in the next room. The person who'd done it either had the guts of a contract killer or they hadn't even thought about the prospect of getting caught. Great. That meant I was either looking for a professional with no qualms about homicide, or an amateur who didn't think through the ramifications of the crime. There weren't any professional killers in Harper's Landing, at least not that I knew of, so that left an amateur acting on the spur of the moment, seizing an opportunity when it presented itself. The choice of the murder weapon dovetailed in with that theory. It was the easiest thing in the world to grab a hammer. The key had to be the soap, in my mind. Why jam it in her mouth? Was the killer trying to shut her up, metaphorically of course, or were they trying to cleanse the victim's words somehow? What else could the gesture mean?

I got to Jean's bed-and-breakfast and admired the carefully scripted wooden sign by the sidewalk. She'd gone with a theme of lavender and maroon, and it was carried out from the sign to the paint on the Victorian to the room decorations. Though it always felt a little formal for my taste, I knew Jean ran her establishment at full capacity most of the time.

The proprietress was at the front desk frowning at a ledger when I walked in. Jean was a slim, handsome woman who had opted for a short haircut in the most unusual way. I'd been at her sixtieth birthday party when she'd declared to the world that she was no longer going to put up with long hair. Janis Farley, the owner and head beautician at Harper's Fine Coifs, came forward with her trusty scissors and combs and proceeded to give the hostess the one thing she'd asked for on her birthday, while we all looked on. Janis had actually blushed as we'd applauded when she was finished.

"That's a healthy frown you've got there," I said.

"Hi, Ben," she said, the lines easing as she saw me. "I was wondering when I'd see you. You didn't have to come down here in person to pay the bill, but I won't turn your money away."

I was embarrassed as I admitted, "I hate to say it, but I didn't come here for that. If you need a check right now, I'll call Mom and she'll have one of the others run it right over."

"Nonsense," Jean said, "I'm doing fine." Her words were spoken as rote, and it was clear she didn't believe them herself.

"Jean, is everything all right?"

She started to say something, then I could tell she changed her mind. "Everything is delightful. So, if you're not here to settle your bill, to what do I owe the pleasure of your company?"

"I need to talk to one of your guests," I admitted. "Would you tell Sharon I'm here?"

She looked surprised by my request. "She checked out two hours ago, Ben. That's why I thought you were here to settle up."

Oh, no. My suspects were disappearing faster than ice cubes on the sidewalk in August. "Did she happen to say where she was going?"

"No," Jean frowned. "Come to think of it, she was in rather a hurry to get out of here. In fact, she left a few things behind. Hang on one second. I'll go get them."

Jean returned a minute later with a suitcase and a garment bag. "These belonged to the contessa. Molly searched through them, but she said there wasn't anything important in either one. Sharon must have forgotten all about them. I didn't care for the woman," she added in a softer voice, as if someone nearby might overhear her.

"Sharon?"

"No, Sharon was a delightful guest. Her employer was

another matter altogether." She bit her lip for a second, then added, "Ben, you know I'm not a prude. Far from it, in fact. But honestly, she was here only one night and she still managed to have two male visitors in her room after hours."

That was interesting. "Did you happen to recognize either one of them?"

"One was a stranger to me, but the odd thing about the other one was that I could swear he was wearing a uniform."

I had a hunch who that might have been. "It wasn't a police officer, was it?"

"Yes, it was," she agreed. "But I didn't know him, and I thought I knew everyone in Harper's Landing."

"He could be a new man on the force," I said, thinking of Brian Ross.

"Perhaps you're right. Honestly, I didn't care for her behavior. She acted as though she was a rock star, not a soapmaker. I shouldn't have said that. I'm sure she was a notable in your profession. I certainly didn't mean any offense by it."

"None taken," I said. "It would have shocked me if you'd known who she was if you weren't a soapmaker."

"Do the police have any idea who killed the contessa?" she asked me.

"If they do, they're not sharing their thoughts with me."

Jean frowned and hesitated before speaking, so I asked, "What is it? You're holding something back, aren't you?"

"Ben, you know how I feel about rumors, but I heard something at the grocery store that you should know about."

"If you're talking about that slash-and-burn article, we already saw the paper. We'll get through it."

"No, that's not it at all." She fiddled with a pendant she

was wearing, then finally said, "I overheard two women say that Diana had every reason to do what she did, that the contessa deserved it. There are quite a few nasty rumors floating around town. I just thought you should know."

"Diana didn't do it," I said with conviction. "I believe in her innocence completely."

Jean patted my hand. "Good for you."

I excused myself from the bed-and-breakfast and walked back to the soap boutique. As I carried the luggage, three different people stopped and asked me if I was going away on vacation. Small towns were deadly when it came to rumors, and I knew that by nightfall all of Harper's Landing would be postulating on why I was ducking out on Diana in her time of need. Let their tongues wag. At the moment, I didn't want to think about what the town's rumor mill was doing to Diana. It gave me just one more reason to find the killer quickly. If folks around town got it into their heads that she was a murderer, no matter what the later facts showed, it would be hard for her to run a business that depended on her customers' good will.

I stowed the suitcase and garment bag in my trunk, then tried to figure out what had happened to Sharon. Where could she be? After our earlier conversation, I had a hard time believing that she'd just bug out like that. Then I remembered what she'd said. Sharon had felt guilty about how expensive Jean's place was, and she'd threatened to move out to the Mountain Lake Motel on her own.

At least it was worth a shot, since I had nowhere else to look for her.

THE daytime desk clerk didn't even need a bribe to tell me Sharon was there. He even gave me her room number without demanding a payoff. I decided he needed lessons in graft and extortion, but I was glad he hadn't had any yet.

Sharon looked surprised to see me when I knocked on her door. "Hi, Ben. Come on in. I was just about to call so I could check in with you."

The décor of the room appeared to be made up of the castoffs from every other midpriced motel in the country. Everything, from the dresser to the desk to the headboard, had an old, used, banged-up look, not that anyone would ever mistake the furnishings for antiques.

"How did you find me?" she asked as she sat on the bed, leaving me the one chair in the room.

"I went by Jean's and she told me you were gone. You didn't have to leave so abruptly."

"Please, I know exactly how much those rooms cost. I wasn't about to stick you with another night's stay on my bill." She looked around the rundown room and somehow managed to say, "This is fine. At least for now."

"I have to admit, for a minute there, I thought you were gone for good."

She looked startled by the idea. "I'm not leaving until the police make an arrest. I told you that."

"A great many people have been telling me a lot of things lately, but you're the only one who seems to be standing by your word."

She shrugged. "I don't know how else to be. So, what can I do for you? I'd offer you a drink, but there doesn't seem to be a minibar here."

"There are a few things I'd like to talk to you about, but there's no easy way to ask the questions I want answered."

She smiled. "Heavens, don't worry about offending me. I'm a big girl, I can take it."

"First off, I understand your employer had two male visitors while she was staying at the bed-and-breakfast."

Sharon shook her head. "That's why I like the anonymity of a motel. Nobody cares who comes and goes."

"Did you know that Connie had visitors?"

"Of course I did," she said. "Their arguments would have been hard to miss hearing."

"What were they fighting about?"

Sharon idly played with the bedspread, and I saw part of it start to unravel. "What does anyone ever fight about? It was love, from the sound of it."

"Do you know who came by?"

"I couldn't miss them; my door was wide open. First Barry came by. He wanted to reconcile, but she wasn't having any of it. Then he started getting nasty, and she threw him out."

"Funny, he told me they were getting back together."

Sharon laughed. "I highly doubt that. Once Connie was finished with a man, that was it. That was what was so odd about the cop who came by. He hadn't given up, either."

"Did you know about him?"

Sharon nodded, then stood and started pacing the room. "She showed me a photograph once and told me that Brian Ross was her first love. He wanted to rekindle things with her, but she actually laughed in his face when he suggested it."

"Why didn't you say anything about this when we talked before?"

She looked contrite. "I was trying to keep them both out of it through some misguided sense of loyalty I had to Connie. I'm sorry I misled you."

"That leads me to my second line of questioning," I said. "I've heard that you were much more to Connie than just her assistant. In fact, there's a rumor going around that you're mentioned prominently in her will and that she fired you."

I was looking for some kind of reaction, but her laughter wasn't the one I'd expected. "Ben, she fired me at least three times a week. Connie had a pretty volatile disposition, so I'd learned to take it in stride. She never failed to apologize the next day whenever she took her frustrations out on me."

That made sense, knowing what I did about the woman. "How about the will? Do you inherit her fortune?"

"I wouldn't know about that," Sharon said abruptly.

"But you told me everything she did was filtered through you," I pushed. "Wouldn't you know exactly what was in her will?"

"Not that," Sharon said. "Connie's personal documents were out of bounds for me. Frankly, I don't give much merit to the rumor that I'm inheriting anything. It was made clear enough that my only pay was for the job I performed." As she stared out the window, she added, "Why don't they just arrest Betsy Blair and be done with it? There's no doubt in my mind she killed Connie."

"How can you be so certain, especially with so many other people around who wished her ill?"

Sharon snorted. "You should have seen the way she confronted Connie here. When Betsy left, she had pure hatred in her eyes."

"I talked to her earlier, and she seemed pretty sane to me. She makes a strong case for her point of view."

That seemed to enrage Sharon. "You've got to be kidding me. You're a soapmaker, but you obviously don't know anything about writing."

"What I saw looked pretty solid," I said.

"You're wrong," she said. "Hang on a second." As she dug through her oversized briefcase, she said, "I found a copy of Betsy's manuscript in Connie's suitcase. What she told me before was true. It's terrible."

"And that's the first time you saw it?" If Sharon had acted as Connie Brown's filter, it appeared that a great deal got past her.

Sharon frowned. "I told you already. Betsy got around me somehow and gave it directly to Connie. I kept telling her she couldn't accept anything from strangers, especially manuscripts, but sometimes she did it anyway. Here it is."

Sharon thrust a thin sheaf of pages at me. It appeared they'd been created on an aging manual typewriter. The impact of each letter varied from nearly piercing the page to barely skimming it, and the ribbon had probably been new thirty years ago. It only took me a second to realize the two documents I'd seen—both sworn to be Betsy's manuscript—were vastly different. So which one was legitimate?

"This isn't the one I saw," I admitted. "Could this version have been faked?"

She snatched it out of my hands. "Are you accusing Connie of something, Ben? I won't have you speaking ill of her, do you hear me?"

"I'm not accusing anyone of anything. Would you mind if I borrowed that? I want to show it to Molly."

She shook her head and stowed it back in her briefcase. "Sorry, but if Betsy still decides to sue, I need it as evidence of just how different this and Connie's book is. Now if you'll excuse me, I'm a little tired right now."

"Of course," I said. Her dismissal was pointed and cool: a rapid descent from the warmth of our earlier conversation. Could that manuscript be the key to the murder? I wanted to see it again, but it didn't look like I'd get that chance without Molly by my side, and I didn't see that happening anytime soon. Speaking of Molly, I wondered if there was any way I could get her to tell me what Connie's will said. If I asked her outright, she'd probably laugh in my face. But what if I brought her some information she didn't already have? I could pass off my acquisition of the knowledge coming from a casual conversation with Sharon, though I doubted it would fool Molly. Still, I had to try. It wouldn't do to call her on her cell phone, though. I'd have to wait until I saw her again, and given the state of her relationship with my brother, the best place to find her was probably at the soap shop, so I decided to head back there.

When I walked back into Where There's Soap, Kate handed me a note. "You need to call this guy back. He sounded pretty upset. What did you do, Ben?"

"Now how could I possibly answer that unless you're a lot more specific than that with your question? I've done any number of things to make people mad in the last few days alone. Sometimes it feels like that's all I ever manage to do."

Kate patted my cheek. "At least you're really good at it."

I looked at the message, but there was just a phone number on it.

"Kate, who exactly was it that called me?"

"He wouldn't give his name," she said. "I asked."

"Fine, I'll call him back in a little bit."

"I wouldn't wait too long," she said. "Just from my little time on the telephone with him, I don't think he's somebody you want to make mad."

I tucked the note in my pocket and went in back to look for Jeff. Jim and Bob were working on the line, making a run of lavender soaps poured in flower molds.

"You guys have the most delicate touch," I said as they pulled soaps from their molds.

Jim snapped, "That's enough out of you, girlie man."

"What's your problem?" I asked him.

Jim explained, "This lunatic actually thinks we should branch out into more spa treatments than Kate suggested, and now you're standing there making fun of my lavender soap. If I had the chance, I'd trade both of you dead even for a car, and then I'd leave it running with the keys in it."

Bob patted Jim on the back. "He's got such a sweet spirit, doesn't he?"

"It's underwhelming," I said. "Have you two seen Jeff lately?"

Jim looked at his watch. "He's late. Having lunch with that ex-girlfriend of yours again. I can't believe how well you're taking the two of them dating." Was it my imagination, or was he disappointed with my reaction?

"Hey, live and let live, you know? As far as I'm concerned, she's not my anything anymore. She and Jeff are starting off fresh, and if something comes of it, they both have my blessing. When they get back, tell Molly I need to talk to her, okay?"

"Sure," Bob said, then he turned to Jim. "Listen, just try the hand lotion. It's great. Feel how soft my hands are already."

Jim said, "When you see me with an earring, an eye patch, and a parrot on my shoulder, then I'll try your hand cream."

"It's not mine," Bob protested. "It's some of the stuff we made with Kate."

"You're wasting your breath," Jim said.

Bob looked at me and said, "Come on, Ben, tell him he can still be manly and use this stuff."

"You're not dragging me into this."

"Coward," Bob said.

"I'd say he's smart," Jim replied.

Kate came hurrying back. I said, "Come here a second, we want you to settle whether it's manly or not to use hand lotion."

She didn't rise to the bait. "Ben, did you call that man back?"

"No, I just got here, remember?"

She frowned. "Well, you don't have to worry about returning his phone call now. He's in the shop, and he's demanding to see you."

I peeked out the door and saw Barry Hill standing near the register with a look of anger on his face. Kate snuck up beside me, with my brothers close behind us both.

"He looks pretty ticked," Jim said. "You want some company?"

"I can handle him," I said.

Bob put a hand on my shoulder. "If you need us, use a code word and we'll come running. Now what should we use?"

Jim said, "How about, 'This guy's getting ready to kick my fanny.' That works for me."

Kate said, "I can tell him you're not here if you'd like me to. That might give him a chance to cool off."

"No, I'll talk to him."

As I approached Connie's most recent ex-fiancé, I said, "I hear you're looking for me."

"Why didn't you return my call?"

"I just got here," I said as I noticed we were garnering some unhealthy attention. "You want to talk about this outside?"

"Is that a threat?" he asked coldly.

"No, it's an invitation to not make a fool out of yourself in front of our customers. If you want to talk to me, I'll be out on the front porch." Maybe I should have stayed where my brothers could help if things did get ugly, but I didn't care. At least if we were both outside, I could shout right back at him, something I was reticent to do in the shop.

He was right on my heels as I stepped outside.

"Where do you get off lying to me?"

I spun around and saw that his fists were clinched.

"I never lied to you," I said. While that wasn't technically true, it was close enough to the spirit of our conversation before to allow me to say it with a straight face.

"You knew who I was all along. After you left, a cop showed up, and I started thinking about how much of a coincidence that was. I started asking around about you, and it didn't take long to track you down."

"So you found me. Why did you want to see me? Did you want to confess to killing Connie? You really should talk to the police about that. I'm sure Molly would be happy to listen to you."

Without warning, he grabbed my shirt with both hands and threw me back against one of the porch supports. The man was stronger than he looked, and there was a sudden violence in his manner that shook me more than I would have ever admitted.

"Get your hands off me," I said as calmly as I could.

"What are you going to do if I don't?"

"Can you really afford to get into any more trouble than you already are?"

That eased his grip some. "What are you talking about?"

"You're right, I told Molly where you were. Believe me, she was going to come looking for you pretty soon anyway, and it would have been a lot harder on you if you'd tried to run. You should be thanking me. I did you a favor."

"Some favor," he said as he released his grip. "You put the law on me."

I straightened out my shirt. "You really should do something about that temper of yours."

"Don't push your luck," he said.

Too bad I was never any good at taking orders. "Is that how you acted around Connie the other night? I heard you two had a fight. Did it turn physical, too? That seems to be the way you deal with your problems."

"We were going to reconcile," he repeated softly. "Do you want to know what we were fighting about? It was your girlfriend."

"How do you even know who my girlfriend is?"

He laughed harshly. "Connie didn't have any trouble figuring that out. That's why she was here, to make amends with Diana Long. They'd already met once the minute she got into town, and they were supposed to get together again after Connie's talk at your little soap store. I told her it was too dangerous, but she insisted that she had to do it to find some peace. I never would have hurt her."

"Not on purpose, I'm sure," I said, though I wasn't sure of that at all. His accusation that Diana was somehow involved threw me, but I kept pushing. "I understand if it was an accident. You got mad, and before you realized what you were doing, she was dead."

He tried to grab me again, but I knocked his hand away this time.

Molly came out onto the porch. As she opened the door, she said, "Ben, I heard you were looking for me." Then she noticed Barry Hill's clenched fists, and mine. "What's going on out here?"

"We were just chatting," I said, trying to will my fists to ease.

"Sure, I believe that," Molly said. She looked at Barry. "I've been looking all over for you. We need to have another talk."

"Now's not a good time for me," he said as he continued to stare at me.

"That's too bad, because it's perfect for me. I'm parked around back. Come on, let's go around the building."

"Fine," he finally said, and turned away from me.

"We can talk later, too," I said.

Molly said, "Oh, don't worry about that. We will."

"I was talking to him," I said, pointing at Barry.

Molly rolled her eyes, and Barry Hill didn't react at all.

I was about to go back inside when I saw some movement on the other side of the street. It was just for a second, but I could swear I saw Brian Ross scurry into the bushes.

Without pausing to consider the consequences, I crossed the street and said, "You might as well come out. I already saw you."

After a few seconds, the cop came out, a look of anger on his face. I was having that effect on a lot of people lately, but that was just too bad.

"How long have you been watching?" I asked.

"I don't know what you're talking about. I thought I spotted a wallet in the bushes, so I went in after it."

"Sure," I said, not even trying to hide the fact that I didn't believe him. "So if you were just walking along, why didn't you stop Barry Hill when he had me pinned against the post?"

"Sorry, I didn't see a thing. It must have happened before I got here," he said.

"Enough of this. You were following one of us. Which one are you after?"

Officer Ross shrugged. "Why would I suspect you of anything?"

"So you were tailing Hill," I said. "I'm curious. Did Connie ask you to keep your eye on him when you were in her room the other night?"

Ross looked at me through hardened eyes. "Now who's tailing who?"

"I'm not following anybody around," I said, though that again wasn't strictly the entire truth. "But this is a small town. People talk. So, what were you and Connie fighting about?"

"We weren't fighting," Ross said. Though his voice sounded calm on the outside, there was a dangerous undertone to it that unnerved me more than Barry Hill's earlier threats. "We were talking about our future."

"From what I understand, Connie Brown wasn't all that fond of revisiting her past."

"You heard wrong," Ross said. "We were working it out. And now somebody's robbed me of that chance. I'm going to find out who killed her."

"And then what are you going to do?" I asked.

"I'm going to handle it," he said simply, "so stay out of my way."

"Somehow I don't think you're going to arrest your suspect once you're sure," I said. "You've got something a little more personal in mind, don't you?"

"I'm finished talking to you," he said. "It would be a lot healthier for you if you minded your own business from now on."

And then he was gone.

I couldn't exactly make him stay. He'd given me some things to think about, but how much of it would Molly listen to from me?

I was about to find out.

NINE

• • •

I watched as Barry Hill sped off with a squeal of rubber. Molly must have spanked him pretty hard. It was time to share my suspicions with her, and see if I could get anything out of her.

"You've got a real gift for ticking people off, Ben," she said as I rounded the corner. Molly was leaning against her patrol car, which was parked beside my Miata. Mom was always happy to have her visit the soap shop—even before she'd started dating Jeff—but she'd been afraid that a squad car parked in the customer lot might give our patrons the wrong idea.

"You're kidding. He was mad at me?" I asked, barely able to contain my grin.

"I don't how you manage to do it."

"What can I say? It's a gift. What did Mr. Hill have to say for himself?"

Molly shook her head. "I'm not telling you that. This is

an ongoing police investigation, Ben, not story time at nursery school."

"Hey, I remember you used to make up great stories," I said.

"That was a long time ago. I'd watch your step if I were you. That man hates you."

"I wish I could say that he's the only one, but unfortunately, he's not alone," I said as I leaned against the Miata. "Your officer Ross has a pretty healthy dislike for me, too. He was out front lurking in the bushes a little while ago, watching my confrontation with Barry Hill. When I called him on it, he made up some lame excuse about spotting a wallet in the bushes, and then he threatened me and told me to butt out of his business."

"What exactly did he say to you?"

I thought about it a second, then admitted, "It was nothing I could quote, but the way he acted toward me was pretty menacing."

"I'll speak with him," Molly said after a brief sigh. "Something came up in my conversation with Barry Hill. It turns out there's more to this situation than either one of us was aware of. Ben, we need to talk about Diana."

"What did he say about her?" I asked. "He's lying, Molly. Diana never talked to Connie."

"How did you know that was what he told me?"

She had me there. "I just assumed as much, since he tried to pass the same lie off to me right before you showed up."

Molly stared at me a full five seconds, then said, "How do you know he's lying, Ben?"

"Don't you think Diana would have told me about it? She was shocked when she found out who the contessa really was. I was standing right there, and so were you."

"Ben, it's not as simple as all that. You need to prepare yourself for some really bad news that might be coming."

"You're not actually going to arrest her, are you? Molly, you're way off on this. Let's go talk to Barry Hill together. I know he'll break down and admit he's lying if we push him a little more."

"I can't just take off and follow your whims," she said. "There are proper procedures I have to adhere to. Don't worry, I'll try to get some corroboration from someone else about Diana's secret meeting with Connie before I do anything about it, but I'm going to find out the truth, no matter who it hurts."

"Fine, if you won't talk to him again, then I'll just have to go myself."

"He hates you, Ben; you realize that, don't you?"

I shrugged. "If he's going to try to pin this murder on Diana, the feeling's mutual."

She looked at her watch, then said, "At least promise me you won't do anything until this evening."

"Why should I wait? If we take too long, he's going to run. I can feel it in my bones."

"Just give me until six, then I'll go with you, though it's against my better judgment. Still, if it's the only way I can keep you from tackling him on your own, I'll tag along."

"I guess I can wait until then."

She moved closer to me, but there was nothing inviting about her stance. "Until I come get you, you're not allowed to even drive past the Lakefront Inn. Do you understand me? If you do, I'll lock you up for obstruction of justice."

"As long as you'll be here by six," I said reluctantly, "I won't go anywhere near him."

"You'd better not," she said.

"And you'd better not arrest Diana without more than that weasel's word."

"Are you threatening me, Ben?" Her words were cold and precise as she stared at me.

"I wouldn't dream of it," I said. "I just don't think her reputation or her business could survive it. All I'm asking for is that you wait until you have the facts."

"That's what I want, too," she said, then got into her squad car and drove off.

I didn't like what I had to do next, but I really didn't have any choice. It was time to talk to Diana and see if Barry Hill had been telling the truth. One of them was lying, and I hoped with all my heart it wasn't Diana. I'd defended her to Molly, but I was putting myself pretty far out on a limb, and I had to be certain that Diana wasn't right behind me, holding a saw.

Rufus was ignoring the store's customers as usual when I walked into Dying To Read. The entire sales counter where Diana usually put bookmarks, postcards, and other announcements about new mysteries was covered with photographic prints.

He looked up as I approached and nodded. "Be with you in a second, Ben."

I was starting to wonder if losing him would be such a blow to Diana's sales after all. He never seemed to do anything store related.

"Diana will be out in a minute. I've got her using the front door now, so that's a step in the right direction, right?"

I lowered my voice. "Where did all your amateur sleuths go? I figured they'd still be hounding her."

Rufus grinned. "They're probably visiting your soap shop of death," he said. "Man, that was some article. They really lit into you guys."

"I'd like to sue them," I said.

"Are you kidding me? You can't buy publicity like that. Your place must be insane."

"Not many folks appear to be willing to risk shopping there," I said.

"Too bad. Hey, while you're here, check this out." He handed his magnifier to me and said, "What does that look like to you?"

It was an image of my family's soap shop at the time of the Soap Celebration. There was no doubt in my mind about the timing of the photograph. I could see the balloons and banners clearly out front. "I thought you were running the bookstore when this was going on," I said.

"Diana asked me to shut down long enough to snap some pictures for you. She thought it would make a nice present. Boy, was she ever wrong."

"So what am I looking for?" I asked as I studied the print. All I saw was the storefront, with people streaming in and out. He'd done some kind of time-lapse photography.

"Check out this guy," he said. "Tell me what's different about him."

"He's the only one not moving," I said after I glanced at it for a second.

"Right on the money. That's kind of whacked, isn't it?"

I was spared from answering when a customer approached. "Excuse me, but I need some help."

Rufus barely looked at him. "Sorry, I'm kind of busy right now."

The man appeared to consider leaving, then he said, "I'm looking for a book by Fredric Brown, but not a single bookstore I've been to has heard of him."

That certainly got his attention. "They've never heard of *The Fabulous Clipjoint*? How about *The Screaming*

Mimis? *What Mad Universe*? What kind of lame places have you been going to?"

"So, do you have something by him?" he asked hopefully.

"No mystery novels," Rufus said, and the man sighed. Then he added, "But we've got a killer anthology. Hang on a second." In a fast pace I'd never seen Rufus use before, he was back with a thick book titled, *From These Ashes*. "Okay, I've got a confession to make. Strictly speaking, these are science fiction stories, but it's every SF short story he ever wrote. This dude was king of the short-short. Trust me. You're gonna love it."

After the customer was gone—his purchase clutched tightly to his chest—Diana came out of the back room. She looked furtively around the room, as if expecting to be mobbed.

"I thought I heard voices," she said as she joined us up front.

Rufus laughed. "They say that's the first step toward insanity. You'd better watch out—you're catching it, Boss."

"Don't let him kid you," I said. "He just made a sale, and from the look of it, it was a nice one."

Rufus blew it off. "No big deal. At least the guy had some taste." He gestured to the photographic array spread out on the counter. "I was just showing Ben the photos I took at the book signing."

"Which one?" Diana asked as she leaned over the counter to look. "These are all of Where There's Soap."

Rufus said, "Okay, maybe I should have said the attempted signing. It's tough to do one without an author. You know, it's the soap thing."

Diana looked a little embarrassed. "Sorry about that, Ben. I thought it would be a nice keepsake of your celebration."

"I appreciate the thought," I said. "Listen, we need to talk."

Rufus said, "Woo, woo, woo. That can't be good."

"In private," I added.

"Come on, Ben, we can chat in my office."

"Spoilsport," Rufus said. As I walked back with Diana, he asked, "Hey, do you want any of these shots?"

Why not? "Sure, I'll take them. Thanks."

"No problem," he said, a phrase I hated. "I'll have them ready for you when you leave." And then he went back to studying the pictures in front of him.

As Diana and I walked back to her office, I said, "I can't believe he doesn't use a digital camera with all the pictures he takes."

"You'd think so, wouldn't you, but he says that digital images lack soul."

I scratched my chin. "His processing bill must be more than he makes here."

"Don't worry about him. His girlfriend's dad owns the camera shop, and he gets his prints for nearly nothing. That's why I'm afraid I'm going to lose him."

"He does seem to know his authors," I said as we walked into her office. "I guess that counts for something."

Diana sat behind her desk and asked, "So what's so urgent, Ben?"

Now that it was time to have our conversation, I wasn't in any mood to talk. "You know what? Let's forget about it for now. It can wait," I said.

"Ben, you can ask me anything. You know that. Go ahead, let's get this over with."

I bit my lip, then blurted out, "There's a witness who saw you talking to Connie Brown the night before she was murdered."

I kept waiting for Diana to deny it, but instead, there was only silence.

"Diana? Is it true?"

"Yes and no," she said as she frowned down at her desk-top.

"How can it be both?"

Diana blew out a puff of breath, then said, "It's true that I talked to her at the bed-and-breakfast the night before the event, but I didn't know who she was. She told me she needed to meet me in person before she would allow me to handle her signing. Believe me, I've had stranger requests from authors than that."

"So what did she say once you got there?"

Diana considered it a moment, then said, "Nothing much, really. It kind of surprised me how quiet she was when I showed up."

"I also heard you were arguing with her."

"That's a lie," Diana snapped. "We barely spoke. Who-ever your source is got it wrong. Is there anything else?"

"Nothing I can think of at the moment," I said. "I'm sorry I brought it up. You just never told me you went over there, that's all. It caught me off guard."

"I don't always tell you everything I do, Ben. Does that surprise you?"

There was a real bite to her words, and I couldn't help myself. I fired right back. "It shouldn't, should it? We don't owe each other anything."

That stung her, and maybe I'd wanted it to a little. She hadn't been completely honest with me, and if there was one thing that was important in a relationship for me, it was trust.

Diana stood, and I could see the pain in her eyes. "Ben, I didn't mean to keep it from you. It just didn't seem all that important before the murder, and afterward I was afraid it made me look guilty. Do you forgive me?"

"There's nothing to forgive," I said. I was being too hard on her—I knew that—but I had no idea how to make it up to her. "Listen, I've got to go."

"What's the rush?" she asked.

"I'm meeting someone in half an hour, and I have to get ready."

She looked at me intently, so I finally added, "Molly's going to let me tag along on something about the murder, and if I'm late, she'll go without me. I want to find the killer as fast as I can, for all our sakes."

"That's what I want, too," she said.

I was at her office door when she added, "Call me later, okay? I don't care how late it is."

"I'll try," I said as I left her. I knew I should have hugged her and told her everything would be all right, but I couldn't bring myself to do it. I was a stubborn and pig-headed man, but blast it all, she should have told me.

I nearly forgot about the photographs as I walked out, but Rufus wouldn't let me. As he handed me a folder with them in it, he said, "Take it easy on her. She's had a rough couple of days."

"So have I," I said.

"The last I heard, nobody's accused you of murder."

"Not recently, anyway," I said. I knew he meant well. "Thanks for the photos."

"My pleasure. I got some good shots of the shop, so if you ever want a print enlarged, I'm your man."

"I'll keep that in mind."

I grabbed a quick sandwich back at my apartment, but I didn't taste a single bite of it. I'd botched things up with Diana, and I was going to have to find a way to make things right again between us. For now, though, I had to meet Molly at the soap shop. I was hoping Barry Hill would be a little more cooperative with both of us there ganging up on him.

It was the best lead I had right now, and I was glad Molly was going with me.

She was twenty minutes late, and I was just about ready to go without her when Molly pulled up in her pickup truck. It was her off duty vehicle, and it took me a second to recognize her.

As she stopped in front of me, the passenger door swung open. "Get in."

"You're not in uniform," I said.

"Are you coming or not?"

I slid in, shut the door, and fastened my seat belt as she took off. "So why the civilian clothes?" I asked. "Not that I mind you in blue jeans and a blouse."

"I'm glad you approve," she said. "I couldn't exactly chauffer you around in a squad car dressed in my uniform. Why else did you think I wanted to wait before we went to see Hill?"

"We have to get one thing clear first," I said as she drove. "It's important that you know this isn't a date. It's strictly business, no matter how much you'd like it to be otherwise." It was all I could do to keep a straight face as I said it.

She laughed, which was the reaction I'd been hoping for. "Don't worry, I wasn't confused by your invitation. Besides, I've already got a boyfriend."

"So I've heard."

She drove a little longer, then said, "Ben, I'm taking a real chance bringing you along with me tonight. Don't make me regret it."

"I'll be good."

"Don't make promises you can't keep," she said, but added a smile to soften her words. "Let me do the talking once we get there, okay?"

"You might as well let me out right now then," I said. "I'm not sure I can keep my mouth shut if I think of something you might be missing." Before she could react to that, I added, "I'm not saying you will, but I won't keep quiet if I think I can help."

She nodded reluctantly. "Fine. Just let me lead off. Can you promise me that much?"

"That I can do."

As we drove on toward the inn, I wrestled with the idea of telling Molly more of the details about Diana's meeting with Connie the night before she died. A part of me felt like I owed my allegiance to my current girlfriend, not my former one. But what if Diana had lied to me about more than that? If she'd snapped and killed Connie Brown, did I really want her to go free? My sense of justice was too strong to accept that. I really had no choice. If she'd committed murder, I would do everything in my power to be sure she was properly punished for it, no matter how I felt about her.

I took a deep breath, then said, "There's something I need to tell you."

"I'm listening," Molly said, never taking her eyes off the road.

"It's about Diana. She admitted to me that she met with Connie Brown the night before the murder. Diana claims she didn't know who Connie was, and I believe her."

"I would expect nothing less from you. You always have been loyal to the people you care about."

"What is that supposed to mean?"

Molly took so long to answer I was afraid she wasn't

going to. When she did speak, there was real sadness in her voice. "Ben, I know how you feel about her, but you should take a step back, at least until we get this resolved."

"I can't do that," I protested. "If I drop her now, how on earth can I go back with her later when she's exonerated?"

"If she ever is," Molly said.

"I don't want to hear that."

"I know, but maybe you need to, anyway. My gut tells me she's involved in this thing up to her eyebrows."

"I don't have to listen to that, either."

We rode the rest of the way in silence. I knew Molly was trying to look out for me, but I didn't have to like it.

Molly and I got to the Lakefront Inn, and there was a crowd there already for dinner, despite, or maybe because of how expensive the place was. I'd eaten there a few times myself in the past, and I envied the diners their experience. We parked in the guest lot and walked toward the guest rooms.

I glanced at Molly and said, "That's a nice purse you've got there. It's kind of big, isn't it?"

She tapped the handbag. "That's because it's got to carry a lot of stuff. I've got my handgun, cuffs, some Mace, and a few other treats, just in case Mr. Hill decides to get a little rowdy."

"Cool. Could I get purses like that for Christmas? I never can figure out what to get my sisters, and that sounds like the perfect accessory for a modern gal's wardrobe."

"Knowing your family, I'm not sure they need the extra help. Be quiet."

She put a hand on my chest and in a second, I heard what had stopped her. A man was yelling fiercely at someone, and I recognized the voice. It was Barry Hill. But who was he shouting at?

Molly motioned me to be quiet as we rounded the corner, but I think we could have been shooting off fireworks for all the impact our arrival made.

Sharon, looking vulnerable and nervous under Barry Hill's glare, was taking a verbal pounding.

"You think you're smart, don't you? Well you're wrong. Don't think you're better than you really are."

Molly stepped out of the shadows, and I was right behind her. "Is there a problem here?"

Barry nearly snapped his neck as he turned toward us, and Sharon took full opportunity of the diversion we were providing.

"I'm so glad you two are here," she said as she hurried over to us.

"I asked you a question," Molly said as she stared at Barry.

"It's not what it looks like. We were just talking."

Molly said slowly, "It sounded like it was more than that to me." Then she turned to Sharon. "Are you all right?"

Sharon shot a quick glance back at Barry. "I'm okay now."

Molly looked at me and said, "Ben, get her out of here so I can have a talk with Mr. Hill, would you?"

"I don't have the Miata, remember?" I said.

"Take my truck," she said as she reached for her keys.

"I've got my car," Sharon said.

Molly looked intently at her and said, "Ben is going to ride back to the motel with you. Is that all right with you?"

"It's fine," she said. Then she leaned in toward me. "Can we just go?"

"Are you going to be okay?" I asked Molly.

She diverted her stare from Barry for just a second. "I'll be better than that as soon as I get you two out of here."

"Call me later," I said as Sharon and I headed back to the parking lot.

I heard Barry say, "I didn't do anything. You can't arrest me for raising my voice."

"Mr. Hill, at the moment you have no idea what I can and cannot do. Now are you going to use a civil tone when you speak with me, or do we have to have this conversation downtown?" Though Molly was dressed in casual attire, there was no mistaking the official tone in her voice. I was more concerned for Barry Hill at the moment than I was for Molly's safety.

Sharon didn't know her as well as I did, though. "Should we stick around, just in case she needs help?"

"Believe me, Molly can handle herself. What was that argument about, anyway? It sounded pretty fierce."

As Sharon opened the door of a lime green Volkswagen Beetle convertible, she said, "He usually sounds that way. Barry's got a terrible temper. I hate it when he yells at me."

I could see her shake a little as I got in the passenger seat. "You're safe now."

"Thanks," she said. "I swear, you always seem to catch me at my most vulnerable. You must think I'm such a baby."

"There you'd be wrong," I said, as she pulled out of the parking lot and headed back to Harper's Landing.

"It's just been such an emotional day for me," Sharon said. "I heard from Connie's business manager this afternoon. It turns out he's the executor of her estate, too, so he had the inside scoop on her will. I know you were curious about that."

"What did he have to say?"

Sharon shrugged. "I'm not supposed to say anything just yet, but I can tell you that the bulk of Connie's estate went to one person. Before you ask, it wasn't me. I've been authorized to stay at the motel until the end of the week, then I'll get a modest settlement. That's it."

"I'm sorry," I said. What else was there I could say?

"It's okay," she said. "I knew this job wouldn't last forever. I just never expected it to end so abruptly."

"What are you going to do after this?"

She stared out at the road for a few seconds, then said, "Maybe I'll go back to school. Or who knows? I might even write a book of my own. I helped Connie with the last few she wrote, and it wasn't that hard." Sharon shook her head. "Listen to me, making all these plans with not much more than a dime to my name. It will all work out, I know that much. After all, it always has so far."

She drove a little more, then said, "Ben, has anybody ever told you that you are an easy man to talk to?"

"I like to listen," I said.

"You're very good at it." She paused, then glanced over at me. "Can you keep a secret?"

"I've been known to hold on to a few over the years," I admitted.

"Your girlfriend Diana is going to get a nice green surprise, and it won't be long."

"You're not talking about Connie's will, are you?"

She grinned, then put one finger to her lips. "Shhh, it's a secret, remember?"

"That's terrible," I said without thinking.

"What's so terrible about inheriting a hundred thousand dollars? If that's bad news, I could use some myself."

I frowned as I turned the ramifications of the inheritance over in my mind. "Don't you understand? When Molly finds out that Diana is going to profit from Connie's death, that's going to make her an even stronger suspect than she already is."

Sharon bit her lower lip. "I never thought of it that way. I'm sorry, I thought I was sharing some good news."

"And it will be," I said, "once this cloud over her is gone. I'll keep your secret."

"I know you will. That's why I told you. Listen, it's silly for you to have to get a ride from the motel to your car. Why don't I drop you off at your apartment, and then I can drive myself back to my room."

It would have been a hassle calling someone to come get me. "Are you sure? I could always follow you back to your room once I have my car."

"Nonsense. Ben, I'm a grown woman. I can handle driving around Harper's Landing all by myself."

I looked over at her, but if there was any doubt in her mind, she didn't show it. "That would be great," I said.

"Good. Then it's settled." She drove on, then said, "I wonder what Barry and Molly are talking about?"

"I doubt it involves the weather," I said. "If it will make you feel any better, I can call you as soon as I hear from Molly."

"You wouldn't mind doing that for me?"

"I'd be happy to," I said.

We were approaching the soap shop, and she pulled into the customer lot. "Your car's not here."

"It's around back. That's where all the family parks."

"Oh, I didn't know that." She looked over at me and said, "Ben, thanks for coming to my rescue tonight."

"I didn't do anything but keep Molly company," I admitted. "She did all the work."

"Don't sell your presence short," she said.

I got out and closed the door. As I did, she said, "See you tomorrow."

"I look forward to it," I said, and she drove off.

TEN

○ ○ ○

SUDDENLY I was in no mood to go back to my empty apartment. I walked back to the front of the soap shop, but no one was there. It was a pleasant evening, so I chose one of the rocking chairs on the porch and stared out at our herb and flower garden.

Usually I was fine with being single and on my own, but I did seem to be happier whenever there was someone else in my life. If Connie Brown had never come to town, as the contessa or as herself, I would be with Diana right now, but that just wasn't possible at the moment. Sharon's admission that Diana stood to inherit a large amount of money because of Connie's death had shaken me more than I realized. After all, Diana was the only one still alive who had been privy to the conversation between her and Connie the night before the murder. While Diana's account seemed reasonable enough, was it the truth? I could envision a much more dramatic confrontation, filled with confessions, pleas, and violent reactions. I wanted to believe Diana with all my heart, but she'd mentioned too many times what a crushing blow losing her parents had been.

But had it been enough to turn her into a murderer? Diana certainly had motive. Since a hammer from our shop had been used in the homicide, the means were present. That left opportunity, and she'd been at the soap shop for the signing. I hadn't kept tabs on her after we'd separated before the actual event, so it was possible she could have slipped into the back room and committed the murder. A chill went through me when I recalled what she said trying to get back into Where There's Soap later. She claimed she'd spilled something on her clothes.

Diana had claimed it was a drink, but could it have been blood instead?

"Stop it," I said to myself out loud. I could easily make a lot of the same accusations of any of my other suspects. With the back door unlocked, anybody could have had access to that hammer and the murder victim, so the means and opportunity were there for all of them.

That left motive. Betsy Blair had reason enough to want Connie Brown dead, if the plagiarism claim was real. Sharon Goldsmith may have thought she was getting more than she did, or her employer could have driven her to the point of murder out of mistreatment, no matter how much she protested that Connie was normally much nicer, and that I'd just seen her in her worst light. Sharon had been a no-show at the signing, something that had struck me as odd at the time. Either Barry Hill or Brian Ross could have killed her as jilted suitors, no matter how many years separated their betrothals to the murder victim.

I wished my grandfather Paulus was in town. It would be good to hash things out with him, but he wasn't in any hurry to get back from his European trip.

I didn't notice the car pull up in the side lot, and I didn't look up until I heard footsteps approach.

I never would have guessed who was paying me a visit.

"May I join you?" Kelly Sheer asked softly.

"Pull up a rocker," I said, gesturing to one of the chairs on the porch.

"I saw you sitting out here as I drove past the shop. Were you talking to yourself, Ben?"

"Maybe just a little," I admitted.

She nodded. Kelly was still dressed in a suit, but I noticed she'd let her hair down, something I'd never seen her do while she was in her "lawyer" mode.

"You're working late," I said.

"Annie and her father are in Charlotte again," she said simply. "It helps me fill the time."

I took it in without comment, since there was nothing I could really say.

"A lot's been happening over the past few days," I finally said. What was wrong with me? This was a woman I'd enjoyed talking to in the past, and our current level of comfort with each other was more like a job interview than a casual conversation.

"More things have been going on than you realize."

"What's that supposed to mean?" I asked.

She started to answer—I could feel it by the way she rocked forward—when I heard my littlest sister's voice. "Is this a private party, or can anyone join in?" Cindy asked.

Her light mood died, and I realized that she must have seen our faces. "Sorry, I didn't mean to interrupt. I forgot my purse."

When she ducked into the shop, Kelly stood. "I'd better be going."

"You don't have to leave," I said.

"Honestly, it's better if I do."

I was still trying to figure her out when Cindy came back. She looked around for Kelly, then said, "I didn't mean to run her off, Ben."

"You didn't," I said. "Do you have a second?"

"For you?" she asked with a smile. "I always have time for my big brother." She moved gracefully into the chair, and I marveled at how my baby sister had grown into such a lovely, poised young woman.

As she settled in beside me, I said, "I'm surprised you don't have a date tonight."

She smiled. "What makes you think I don't?"

"Don't let me keep you then," I said. "I know how impatient your young men tend to get when you keep them waiting."

"It's good for them to get a little antsy," she said, settling back in her chair, obviously in no hurry. "So, what's up with the murder investigation? Can you believe the newspaper? We should sue them. I can't believe everything turned out the way it did. What are you going to do next?"

I grinned over at her. "Which question would you like me to answer first?"

"Take your pick," Cindy said. "I've got the time."

"The investigation is taking more turns than a drive in the mountains. Every time I think I've got my finger on who killed Connie Brown, something happens to make me doubt my earlier choice."

She rocked a few seconds, then said, "It can't help that Diana is a suspect. Does Molly really think she might have done it?"

I shrugged. "Molly Wilkes is a real pro, no matter what some folks in Harper's Landing might think. She goes by evidence, not her idea of what the truth might be. The two of us have had our share of differences in the past—the whole world knows that well enough—but I trust her. She'll figure out who did it."

Cindy pinched my arm. "Along with a little help from my oldest brother. Ben, she relies on you more than either one of you will admit. I know how much you like to snoop." She rocked a few seconds more, then asked, "Why did you become a soapmaker and not a cop?"

"Soap is in my blood," I said. "I can't imagine ever doing anything else. I might dip my toe in the detecting water now and then, but I could never do what Molly does." I paused my rocking long enough to ask, "Speaking of career choices, how is your decision coming? Any ideas on a career path?"

She shook her head. "I don't know what to do. Soapmaking is fun, but do I really want to spend the rest of my life making seashells and turtles, and teaching people how to enhance their homemade soap? How fulfilling could that be?"

"You'd be surprised," I said, careful to keep my voice neutral.

"Ben, I didn't mean anything by that. You know I respect the family business. I'm just not sure it's for me. I'm sorry if I offended you."

"Littlest sister, you'd have to do a lot more than that to bother me. I know soapmaking might not be for everybody, but I love doing it. I thought you enjoyed teaching classes."

She shrugged. "I do. I'm just not sure it's all I ever want to do."

"I understand," I said, "but we're not that rigid around

here. Work with us until you figure out what you want to
do with your life."

"No thank you. It would be too easy to get sucked into
the family business forever. I can just see waking up right
here thirty years from now and wondering how I let it happen."

"Ultimately," I said, "we all have to make that decision
for ourselves. I'm glad you're giving this a year's trial, but
it's going to be up soon. If you're eager to get out, you
should probably make a break for it soon before we get our
claws all the way in you."

Cindy rocked forward and stood up.

"Hey, I was just joking," I said as I looked up at her.

She smiled slightly. "I know, but you're right. It's time I
made a decision. I just don't want to disappoint the family."

"And by family, you mean Mom, don't you?"

"She's a big part of it," Cindy admitted.

"Choose your path and live it to the fullest. If you give it
anything less than everything you've got, that's the only
way Mom will ever be disappointed in you. We all love
you, and nothing would delight the entire family more if
you found a niche here with us, but we all want you to be
happy. That's what's important."

"Thanks, Ben," she said softly. There was a somber
mood between us, and it was pretty obvious that Cindy felt
it every bit as much as I did. She added lightly, "So, are
you going to sit out here all night, or are you going home?"

"I think I'll stay awhile longer," I said. "But you don't
have to keep me company. Go on, you've kept your date
waiting long enough."

She leaned down and kissed my cheek. "Thanks for the
talk."

"Anytime," I said.

I'd meant every word I'd said to her. It wasn't a requisite that family members work at Where There's Soap. It had just turned out that way. But if Cindy wanted to go out in the world and find her own way, I'd do my best to support her. I'd made a vow to myself that I'd watch out for her the day she'd been born, and I wasn't about to break it now.

I decided I'd sat around on the porch long enough. I wasn't in the mood for company, so I drove my Miata to my apartment and made myself another sandwich. I wasn't getting much nutrition in the way of fruits or vegetables lately, but I wasn't a big fan of cooking a big meal when it was just me. Maybe I'd go out and get a strawberry milkshake later. That ought to satisfy a couple of the food groups, fruit and dairy, too. As much to keep me company as anything else, I flipped the television on and looked for some sporting event to take my mind off my problems.

All I could find was a soccer match on one of the Spanish channels.

It would have to do. As I ate my peanut butter and jelly, I tried to match the excitement of the announcers with the events unfolding on the field, but it was too taxing. My two years of high school Spanish were long gone and mostly forgotten, but every now and then I'd pick up a word or two that I recognized.

There was a knock on my door, and I was surprised to find Molly there.

"Come on in," I said as I stepped aside. "Would you like a sandwich?"

She sneered at my PB&J. "I don't think so. Your brother's taking me out tonight. I just wanted to pop in and find out what Sharon told you."

"Are we actually comparing notes now?" I asked. I turned the soccer game off, but not before getting an odd look from Molly.

"We'll see," she said. "It depends on what you've got."

I nodded. "Fair enough. I asked Sharon what they were fighting about when we showed up, but she was kind of vague."

"So was Barry. I'm usually pretty good at reading people, but I couldn't quite get him tonight. To be honest with you, I thought he acted just a little bit scared."

"Do you think he's afraid of being caught? He could have killed Connie, you know," I said. "Your instincts are usually pretty good at this stuff."

"But not always," she said. "I'm not ready to commit one way or the other just yet. Did you manage to get anything from her?"

I'd been dreading sharing what I knew, but Molly would find out soon enough. Maybe I could spin it so it didn't look so bad. "Sharon told me she talked to Connie's executor. Diana's going to inherit a fair chunk of money from the estate. It's atonement money from the car accident, I guess."

"That's interesting," Molly said.

"It doesn't make Diana a murderer," I said a little louder than I'd intended to.

"It doesn't exactly clear her, either. How much is she getting? Did Sharon say?"

"She told me, but I still don't think it's relevant."

Molly shook her head. "Just tell me, Ben."

"It's a hundred thousand dollars," I said softly.

Molly whistled. "That's certainly a motive for murder."

"She didn't do it," I said stubbornly, and the words sounded hollow even to me. I hated giving Molly another reason to think of Diana as a killer, but she'd find out sooner or later, and at least if I told her, I could try to downplay it.

Molly didn't comment one way or the other as she asked, "Did you find anything else out?"

I tried to keep my temper in check. "Sharon's got permission to hang on here awhile, then she'll be discharged with a token severance. From the sound of it, she's not getting much."

"What else did she tell you?"

"That was really about it," I admitted. "I don't guess it's much, is it? Oh, there was one more thing. She wanted me to call her after I talked to you."

"Whatever for?"

"To be honest with you, I think she's curious about what Barry told you."

Molly appeared to think about that for a few seconds. "Tell her he wouldn't budge. No, on second thought, say that I wouldn't tell you, but it seemed like I was holding something back. Can you do that?"

I nodded. "That shouldn't be too difficult, since I suspect you are."

She smiled. "You're funny, have I told you that lately? Ben, I'm trying my best to come up with a suspect other than your girlfriend. I figure if I stir things up enough with all of my candidates, one of them might slip up. Otherwise, I'm going to focus on Diana."

I shook my head. "It's amazing to watch a professional police investigation in action. What happened to tracking down clues with magnifying glasses?"

"I left mine at home," she said. "No matter what they show on television, forensics can only do so much. It nearly always comes down to people, and the ways they react to different stimuli. A push here and a nudge there can work wonders that no crime lab can come up with. If Sharon acts the least bit out of character when you tell her, let me know. I gave Barry Hill a twist as I was leaving, and I'm curious to see how he might react."

"What about Brian Ross?" I asked, well aware I was on delicate ground. "Have you poked him at all?"

"Are you still on that kick?" she asked. "He's a decent cop and a nice guy, Ben. I can't imagine he's a killer."

"I can't accept the possibility that Diana is one either," I said, "but I keep telling you things that could end up burying her."

Molly frowned for nearly a full minute, then she retrieved a police radio from her purse.

"Sarah, it's Molly. Do you have a twenty on Brian Ross?"

"He's covering the downtown beat tonight," a woman's voice replied.

"Thanks. Keep this between us, okay? I don't want anybody to know I was asking." She turned off the radio. "There, that should do it."

"Are you going to go talk to him now that you know where he is?"

Molly grinned. "I don't have to. Sarah won't be able to keep her mouth shut. Brian probably already knows I was asking about his whereabouts."

"Molly, I don't want you taking any chances on my account."

"Ben, I don't believe Brian Ross had anything to do with Connie Brown's death, so I'm not putting myself in danger."

"Still, I'd feel better if you'd promise to watch your back."

"I've been doing it so long it's a matter of habit now." She walked to the door, then said, "Stay out of trouble yourself, would you? I'd like to have one evening where I don't have to save you or one of your family members from imminent danger."

"That sounds like something that would be good for me, too," I said. "Tell Jeff I said hi."

"Let's just assume I won't and be done with it," she said, and then left.

I looked up the number for Sharon's motel, then asked for her room. She picked up on the first ring.

"Hi, it's Ben. I promised you I'd touch base, and Molly just left."

"Thanks for calling. So, what did she find out?"

"She was a little guarded," I said, trying not to make the truth sound like a lie. "I wish I could say more, but she was pretty closemouthed about the whole thing."

"That's fine," Sharon said. "I was just wondering what Barry might say. When he's drunk, it's hard to tell what he'll come up with."

"Does he get that way very often?"

"Every time I've seen him lately, he's had bourbon on his breath. I'm worried about what he might do."

She really did sound concerned. I said, "Maybe you should move to another motel. You could register under another name, and I doubt he'd be able to find you."

"I'm safe enough here. Barry thinks I'm still at the bed-and-breakfast. Thanks for calling, Ben. Good night."

"Good night," I said. I thought about calling Molly and updating her on what Sharon had said, but there really wasn't anything to tell.

I flipped the soccer game back on, then grabbed a book and started reading. It couldn't hold my attention though, and I finally turned the television off, too. It was hours before I could go to bed without waking up at five a.m., but I was bored beyond description. I decided what I needed was a drive in my Miata, and though the night air had chilled somewhat, it was time to take the top down and let the sights and smells of the night get rid of the staleness in my mind.

I pulled out into the darkness, enjoying the anonymity the nighttime brought. I drove through town, passing under the streetlights of Main Street like spotlights on a stage, illuminating a small, moving disk of pavement, one after the other. Then I was out on the highway again, heading toward Hunter's Hollow without any plan or design.

Route 127 was a two-lane road, with vast open spaces between the two towns. On a beautiful day, full of sunlight and fresh breezes, I'd push the Miata up toward sixty, though the posted limit was forty-five. There were enough curves in the road to make it feel like I was going over a hundred.

Tonight was a time for caution, though, not exuberance. I had the road mostly to myself when I spotted a pair of headlights coming up fast from behind me. The high beams nearly blinded me as the car approached, and I automatically pushed the accelerator even harder to the floor. Still, my tail was there, gaining on me by the second. I tried to glance back to see if I could get some idea who was back there, but the blinding lights obscured it all.

Then I felt the first nudge, and the Miata surged forward on its own. I'd been braced for a real impact, and the delicate touch startled me. The second time the driver hit me, the force of the blow nearly knocked my small sports car off the road. I had to fight the Miata's inclination to go straight when the road curved.

That's when I got it. Someone was trying to shove me into the woods near the road. There were copses of trees everywhere, with only small breaks in between. A massive pine or oak would destroy my car at the speed I was going, and most likely kill me instantly. A seat belt could only do so much. With white-hot fear gripping me, I knew if there was a third collision, I was going to die. I couldn't call for help, and I couldn't defend myself. All I could do was try to outrun the vehicle behind me.

Grabbing my seat belt strap, I pulled it as tight as it would go and rammed the accelerator to the floor. If I was going to die tonight, it was going to be on my own terms.

The tires skidded a couple of times as I came precariously close to the gravel shoulder, but the car behind me kept coming. I had to do something drastic.

It was time to put it all on the line.

I punched the gas to the floor, steered the car toward the middle of the road, then raced for the safety of Hunter's Hollow. Hitting the town limits wouldn't necessarily mean that I was out of danger, but I was hoping that with witnesses around, the attempted murderer would be forced to give up.

The lights behind me suddenly vanished, and I wondered if the car that had been pursuing me had run off the road. I pulled over, caught my breath when I realized I was alone, and then did something that in retrospect was pretty stupid.

I turned the Miata around and headed back to Harper's Landing. I dialed Molly's number on my cell phone as I drove. "Sorry to interrupt your date," I said before she could say a word, "but somebody just tried to kill me."

"What happened?" Molly asked.

I told her, and she said, "And you're driving back into

town? Pull over right now. I'll send a car out there, and Jeff and I will be out in a few minutes. Don't do anything stupid," she added.

"You mean anything else? Don't worry, I'll be right here."

I hung up the phone and decided to see how much damage had been done to the back of the car. When I tried to stand, though, my legs nearly buckled and I collapsed back into my seat. The confrontation had weakened me much more than I'd realized.

By the time the first squad car found me, I'd managed to get my composure back, and my ability to walk.

I got out and greeted the patrolman, happy to see that it wasn't Brian Ross. Where was he? I wondered. Ditching the car he'd used to try to kill me, or off on some completely innocent activity?

"Are you all right, sir?"

I'd grown used to being called sir, but that didn't mean I had to like it. "I'm Ben Perkins," I said as I held out my hand.

"I know who you are," he said with a smile. "You don't remember me, do you?"

It was tough to see his face in the weak light coming from his headlights. "Sorry, I don't."

"That's okay," he said, laughing. "My name's Shawn. I dated your sister Cindy a few times in high school."

"You'll have to be more specific than that," I said.

He nodded. "She's a sweet girl. I know she's got a lot of fans." He shined his light on the back of my car. The damage wasn't nearly as bad as I'd expected. "Looks like they clipped your bumper pretty good, but a good body man could probably fix it."

"I'm just glad that's all the damage it did. You might

want to go look for whoever tried to run me off the road. I've got a feeling they hit a tree somewhere back there."

"I didn't see anything driving over here," he said. "Besides, I've got my orders. I'm to stay with you until Officer Wilkes gets here."

"Molly always was too overprotective of me," I said. "Go on. I'll tell her it was my fault."

He was about to argue the point when Jeff pulled up, with Molly beside him. As they got out, I said, "I'm sorry about this. I didn't mean to interrupt your date."

"Don't be nuts," Jeff said. "Are you all right?"

"I was a little shaky at first, but I'm fine now. Molly, you should let Shawn go look for the car that did this. I've got a bad feeling in my gut they ran off the road."

She nodded to him. "Go on. I've got this covered."

Shawn disappeared in his squad car, and Molly said, "Tell me what happened."

"I was just driving along, and all of a sudden some maniac came up from behind and started tapping my bumper. I drove as fast as I could, and the next time I looked up, the headlights had disappeared."

"Can you describe the vehicle?"

"All I saw were headlights," I admitted. "It happened too fast, and the high beams blinded me. I thought you-all were cracking down on drunk drivers."

"What makes you think the other driver was drunk?" Molly asked.

"Who else would try to bump me off the road?"

Molly shrugged. "You've been asking a lot of questions about Connie Brown's murder. Maybe you're getting too close to the truth."

"That's crazy," I said. "You know as well as I do that I don't have a clue about who killed her."

"We both realize that, but does the killer? Ben, I want to put a man on you until we clear this up."

"Absolutely not," I said. "I'm sure you're wrong."

"But what if I'm not?"

Jeff said, "Listen to her, Ben. What could it hurt?"

"My spirit, my pride, my shell of a love life, just about everything," I said. "If I start running from shadows, I'll be afraid to leave my apartment."

"Talk some sense into him," Jeff told Molly. "He never did listen to me."

"And you honestly think he'd listen to me?" Molly asked.

"It was just some drunk," I said. "You both are being paranoid, and as soon as Shawn reports back in, you're both going to see that I'm right."

Just then Molly's radio squawked. "No sign of anybody off the road anywhere near here," he said.

"Are you sure?"

"I checked twice. If there's a crash anywhere around here, they went so far back into the woods that I can't see them."

"Keep looking anyway," she said.

"Yes, ma'am."

"I don't get it," I said. "They were right behind me. How could they just disappear like that?"

"How indeed?" Molly asked. She looked at the Miata, then added, "It doesn't look like your car was too badly damaged."

"The bumper got banged up, but it's nothing I can't live with for now. I just wish I knew where they went."

She stared at me a second, then asked, "Are you all right?"

"Why does everybody keep asking me that?" I rubbed

my face and was surprised to see that my hands were both shaking.

"Why don't I drive your car home for you?"

"I'm not an invalid," I said. "I can drive myself."

"At least let Jeff and me follow you," she said.

I wasn't about to admit to them that I was still a little shaky, even if I did manage to look calm on the outside. "You both are going to make a fuss about it, so I guess it wouldn't hurt anything."

I managed to drive home without incident, and Molly and Jeff honked and waved as they left me.

I needed a shower, and the hot water soaked my tired muscles as I let it beat down on me. Could Molly be right? Had the confrontation been more than just an angry drunk looking for trouble? If I'd managed to shake things up enough to get someone to want me dead, why didn't I know what I'd done?

I went to sleep with more questions than answers, but that really wasn't anything new in my life.

Tomorrow, I'd have to see if I could push things a little harder. It was the best way to get the killer to crack.

But I'd watch my back in the meantime, just in case Jeff and Molly were right. I wouldn't be able to do anybody any good if the killer managed to get to me before I exposed whoever it was out there with homicide on their mind.

ELEVEN

○ ○ ○

THE next morning I could barely get out of bed. I didn't think the impacts of the car hitting me from behind had been that forceful, but I ached all over. Then I realized that I'd most likely done some of the damage myself. My entire body had been clinched in fear as I'd tried to elude the other driver, and I must have strained muscles I'd forgotten I'd even had. After a long and hot shower, a couple of Tylenols, and a big breakfast, I was finally feeling like myself again. As I approached my car, I inspected the Miata's back bumper again, this time in sunlight.

It wasn't as bad as I'd feared, but I knew I couldn't live with the damage, even though it probably wasn't even structural. I loved my sports car, and I couldn't bear to see it beat up or dented in any way. I'd have to call Harry at Auto Finesse and see if he could fit me in. No doubt he'd have some classic he was restoring that I could borrow until the Miata was repaired. He'd sold the Mustang I'd rented from him before after fixing it up, but I knew there was always another project for him.

For now, though, it was time to go to Where There's Soap until I could figure out what my next move was.

Every sister was waiting for me in the boutique area of our shop when I walked in. I knew they were there for me by the similar expressions on their faces.

"Ben, you can't keep taking chances like that," Cindy said.

"Yeah, you're not bulletproof," Louisa added.

"Though you like to think that you are," Kate finished.

I shook my head as I looked at them, each in their turn. "Is that the best you can do? Where are the guys? And why isn't Mom out here with you?"

Louisa admitted, "Once our other brothers found out you were all right, with minimal property damage, they lost interest in what happened last night."

Cindy said, "That's not true, and you know it. I'm sure they're all eager to hear about your exploits. Don't lie to them too much, Ben. You know how they get."

"Boys will be boys, won't they? Mom's not in yet," Kate added. "She's going to be late."

"You're kidding me," I said. "She's never late."

"Don't you think we know that? That's why we're worried about her," Cindy said. "She was awfully mysterious yesterday when she told us she wouldn't be here in time to open the shop."

I walked past them. "It sounds like she's the one you three should be worried about, not me." I didn't know what Mom was up to, but if it meant some of the intensity of my sisters' normal scrutiny was deflected away from me, I would do my best to take advantage of it.

I wanted to go to my office, since it was a great place to

think, but that meant I had to go through my brothers in back.

"I told you he was okay," Jeff said, then turned to me. "They didn't believe me."

"It's not like you haven't exaggerated things before," Jim said.

Bob came to his defense. "That happened when he was in the third grade. When are you going to get over it?"

Jim scratched his chin. "Maybe in another year or two." He looked me up and down, then asked, "How bad is the Miata?"

"Bad enough to need a new bumper," I admitted. "Jeff, have you talked to Molly this morning?"

He got my meaning instantly. "She said they didn't find a single trace of the car that tried to run you off the road. It was as if the thing vanished into thin air."

"Like I said, it was probably just a drunk driver."

Bob put a hand on my shoulder. "So what exactly happened?"

"Some maniac kept trying to clip me from behind, but I floored it and got away."

Jim said, "Man, I would have loved to be riding beside you when you did that. How fast did she go?"

"I didn't have time to look down at the speedometer," I admitted, "but I was flying. You've got to be careful on the roads these days. There are maniacs everywhere."

"One less than usual right now, since you're here," Jim said with a grin.

"I can't argue with you there. It's no big deal, guys. A drunk got mean, and I was the only target around."

I left them debating the merits of that particular theory as I headed upstairs to my office. I walked in, put my feet up on my desk, and tried to decide what I was going to do next.

There was a knock at my door a minute later, and Louisa walked in. "Ben, Mom just called. She's not going to be able to make it in time for the private lesson she scheduled for this morning, and she wants you to teach it."

"Why can't somebody else do it?" I asked. I was intent on solving Connie Brown's murder, and I didn't want to take a second away from it if I could help it.

"Why, because you're so busy?"

"Believe it or not, I am. I'm thinking," I said.

"I know how taxing that must be for you, but we're tied up with inventory. It's enough trouble to stop when a customer comes in, but we need all three of us to do it right. I guess one of the guys could teach the class in a pinch."

"I don't think so," I said as I started to stand. My brothers were not great teachers, as a rule. "What's the class? Basic Soapmaking?"

"No, this woman already knows how to make soap. She's interested in botanicals."

While I was proficient enough with the plants we used in our soapmaking, botanicals were Mom's specialty. I'd have to muddle through somehow. "Fine, I'll teach it. When does it start? I need a little time to brush up on my notes."

Louisa smiled at me. "You'd better make it quick, then. Your pupil is downstairs in the classroom waiting for you."

I shook my head as I hurried past her. "Thanks for the advance notice."

"Thank Mom, don't thank me," Louisa said.

I found a prim, middle-aged woman with a notebook in one hand and a pen in the other waiting for me in the classroom.

"I'm Ben Perkins," I said as I offered to shake her hand.

"My name is Opal Blake." She looked at my extended

hand as if it were covered in slime. "I was expecting a woman."

"Sorry to disappoint you, but I'm perfectly qualified to teach you whatever you need to know." That was a stretch, but I knew just enough about every part of the soapmaking process to be dangerous. "Of course, if you'd like to reschedule your private session, I'd be more than happy to set you up with another teacher at a different time."

She frowned, bit her lip, then finally shook her head. "No, that's all right. I suppose you'll do."

I didn't take offense. I took her mild lack of enthusiasm as a challenge, and I was more than up to it.

"Very good," I said. "Let's start with the *a*'s, shall we? I don't suppose you'd count almond meal or oil, so we'll begin with aloe vera gel. We have anise oil, apricots, avocados, buttermilk—"

"That's not what I wanted to know," Opal said plaintively. "Didn't anyone tell you what the session was supposed to cover? How on earth can you teach me when you don't even know the subject matter?"

"I'm sorry; I understood you were interested in the botanical products used in soapmaking."

She scowled at me as she said, "I can read a book if I want to know all that, or even study your shelves." She shifted her disgruntled gaze to the shelf of additives I'd been reading from, then offered me another look of complete contempt.

There was only one thing I could do. I had to press on, no matter what woman's opinion of me was. "So tell me, Opal, what exactly would you like to know?"

"I'm interested in seeing the actual plants, not the processed oils. Can you do that?"

"Absolutely," I said. "Let's go out into the garden."

"That's more like it," she said.

I walked with Opal out of the classroom, through the boutique—stopping to give Louisa a frown along the way—then led my student outside to our herb and flower plot.

I led her to the edge of the garden, reached down and plucked a small, needlelike leaf. "This is rosemary," I said as I handed it to her. "For our purposes, it's used to treat acne, dandruff, asthma, poor circulation and to soothe nerves. Some folks even believe it promotes hair growth."

I knelt down to the bed beside it and retrieved a small, fan-shaped leaf.

When I handed it to her, she asked, "And what's this?"

"Rub it between your hands, then smell it," I instructed.

"It's peppermint," she said, startled by the revelation.

"On the nose," I said. "We've got a dozen other mints growing here. It happens to blend well with rosemary, but it's important not to use too much of it."

"I love the scent. It reminds me of my grandfather. What happens if you overdo it?"

"Do you mean besides the overwhelming smell? It can irritate your skin, and we frown on anything that can do that here. A soap should offer comfort and respite, not discomfort."

"What's that over there?" she asked as she pointed to a bed of chamomile.

"That's a plant that's been used since the time of the Egyptians. It's not just good for soapmaking. It will lighten your hair, help a toothache and it also makes a great cup of tea. Any guesses?"

"I never guess," she said formally. "I must know. That's why I'm here."

"Okay, then I'll tell you. It's chamomile."

I heard a pair of high heels clicking toward us and saw my mother approach, loaded down with packages. She thrust them at me as she said, "Mrs. Blake, I'm so sorry I'm late."

"Was there some kind of emergency?"

Mom shrugged. "My watch battery died at the most inopportune time. I'd be happy to step aside if you'd like so you can continue the lesson with my son, or I'd be equally pleased to take over."

Opal Blake looked at me, then said, "No offense intended, Mr. Perkins, but if you wouldn't mind, I'd like to switch teachers."

"I'm not offended at all," I said, letting some of the relief I felt slip onto my face. "You're in good hands."

"Thank you, Benjamin," Mom said, then turned to her student. "Now, where were we?"

"Chamomile," Mrs. Blake said primly.

I left them to it and walked back inside. The first sister I saw—who happened to be Kate—got the packages. "These are Mom's. She's teaching my student now, and I have to go out."

"Playing hooky already? It's a little early in the day, isn't it?" Kate asked with a smile.

"Hardly. I'm looking for a murderer."

She nodded somberly. "I shouldn't have teased you. Good luck, Ben."

I accepted that, then said, "I just wish I didn't need so much of it."

I got into the Miata and drove off before I was shanghaied into another soapmaking task. It was time to take a more active role in finding Connie's murderer, and I knew I'd been holding back in deference to Diana. That was the wrong thing to do, because I wasn't giving it my full effort.

Maybe it was because I was afraid of what I might find out. Whatever happened, I had to believe in my heart it would be better knowing the truth than suspecting a darkness within my girlfriend that might not even be there.

I needed to talk to Diana, and this time, I was going to have to ask her some very hard questions.

I found Rufus taking photographs in front of Dying To Read when I got there. He looked oblivious to the world as he studied the shop through his lens.

"Is your boss inside?" I asked him.

He looked startled to see me. "Man, you've got to stop sneaking up on me like that."

"Sorry," I said. "I didn't think I was being particularly stealthy. Is Diana inside?"

"No, she's at her aunt and uncle's place. You know where that is, don't you? I'm the only one working here, until she tells me different."

I gestured to the bookstore. "If you're out here, then who's inside waiting on customers?"

He shook his head. "We haven't had anybody come by all morning. What sense does it make for me to sit inside when there's nobody there?"

At that moment, the bookstore's front door opened and a timid little man stepped out. "Excuse me, but do either one of you work here? I've been waiting at the counter for ten minutes to buy this book, but no one seems to be inside."

"I'll be right with you," Rufus said, and the man ducked back in. Rufus looked defiantly at me and said, "So, one guy slipped past me. It's no big deal."

As he walked in to ring up the sale, Rufus asked, "Should I call Diana and tell her you came by looking for her?"

"No, I'll talk to her later myself. Thanks."

"Yeah," he said as he went back into the bookstore. His vigilance and dedication to his work was actually slipping, if that were possible, but that was Diana's problem. Or at least one of them.

I decided to drive out to Hunter's Hollow and talk to Diana and her aunt and uncle at the same time. I'd wanted to ask them about their own alibis for the time of the murder. After all, they'd lost two people they'd loved, too.

Diana looked shocked when she answered the door at the Long's house. She was barefoot, and wore blue jeans and an old football jersey sporting a bulldog and a big *82* on it.

"Ben, what are you doing here?"

"I need to talk to you," I said.

"Look at the way I'm dressed," she said. "I wasn't expecting you."

"I didn't know you played football," I said with a smile, trying to break some of the tension that still hung between us.

"It belonged to an old boyfriend from high school. I caught him flirting with another girl, so I kept his jersey after I broke up with him. Listen, I'm not happy about the way we left things the last time."

"I'm not either," I said.

The look of relief on her face was only temporary as I added, "But there are some questions that need to be asked, and until they are, there's going to be a big wall between us. You don't want that, do you?"

"You know I don't," she said, "but I'm not sure why you're digging into this so hard. Why don't you let Molly handle it like you said you were going to do?"

"Because the murder occurred in my shop," I said, "and

if I hadn't invited Connie Brown to Harper's Landing, it never would have happened here at all."

"Ben, you can't blame yourself," she said softly.

"I'm not, but I'd be a fool to think that I'm not at least somewhat responsible. Diana, I need the truth."

"I've never told you anything else," she said.

"I consider omission as big a sin as commission."

"You know what? Maybe it would be better if you left after all." The affection in her voice that I'd felt in the past was gone now.

"I'm not going anywhere without answers," I said.

"What do you expect me to say, that I killed her? I didn't, but if I'd known who she was before that signing, I might have." Diana's eyes flared as she added, "She killed my parents. She deserved to die."

I couldn't believe this was the same sweet woman I'd been dating. At that moment, I fully believed that Diana was capable of killing Connie Brown, something I hadn't been able to visualize at all since the murder.

Suddenly behind her, Mr. and Mrs. Long showed up. Diana's uncle said, "Ben? Is that you? Invite him in, Diana. What's wrong with you, girl, have you lost all your manners?"

"Ben can't stay," she said. "He was just leaving."

"Actually, I have a minute or two," I said, trying to ignore the daggers in Diana's glare.

"Excellent," Mrs. Long said. "Come in and have some tea."

I stepped past Diana and walked into the living room. It was a shrine to Diana, with photographs from every year of her life, and events with the most trivial significance were treated with reverence and awe. The Longs hadn't been able to have any children of their own, and when they took Diana in, every ounce of their parental desires apparently flooded out onto her. It was a wonder she could survive it without becoming the world's biggest narcissist.

"I'll be right back with a tray," Mrs. Long said.

"Thanks, but I don't need any tea. What I really came here for are answers."

Diana said, "Ben, I told you, I'm done discussing this with you."

"You're not the only one who could be involved here," I said.

It took Diana's uncle a second to get it. "You're talking about that woman's murder, aren't you?"

"I am," I said.

Mrs. Long said, "Ben, you can't think Diana had anything to do with that, can you?"

Her husband patted her hand. "He's talking about us, too, dear."

"That's it," Diana said abruptly. "Ben, you're leaving. You're not welcome here anymore."

I stood, but as I started to leave, Mr. Long said sadly, "Not that we need to tell you anything, but my wife and I were in Charlotte the entire afternoon on the day of the murder."

"Can you prove that?" I asked.

"I can and I have," he said. "I've already told the police from Harper's Landing, but I'm not going to satisfy your whim without more reason than you've given me. Diana was right. It's time you left."

Mrs. Long scowled at me as I stepped past her toward the door. It appeared that I was three for three in offending the Longs. As I walked out to the Miata, I saw Diana staring at me through the front window. She was crying—I could see it from there—but I didn't have any comfort to offer her.

I was more upset by the confrontation with Diana and her family than I cared to acknowledge. While it was true that I might not have had the right to ask the hard questions, some-one had to, and I'd been under the impression that no one had. After our conversation though, it was pretty obvious that Molly had already interviewed Mr. and Mrs. Long. I just wished she would have shared that particular tidbit with me.

On the other hand, I had to admit that I was starting to see how Molly could think that Diana could have done it. One look in her eyes was all I'd needed to confirm that I couldn't rule her out as a suspect, no matter what my rela-tionship was with her. But while there were other possibil-ities, I was determined to focus on them.

As I drove toward home, I considered everyone else I believed was motivated enough to commit murder. Sharon Goldsmith, Betsy Blair, and Barry Hill were all on my list; Brian Ross was on it, too.

If Diana had murdered Connie Brown, did I really want to be the one who proved her guilt? I would do it if I had to, but not until I'd exhausted every other suspect on my list.

Barry Hill's temper had bothered me from the first time I'd heard him snarl. He had been in the middle of a con-frontation with Sharon when Molly and I had shown up. But what had they been fighting about? It had appeared to me that Barry was threatening Sharon in some way, but she hadn't said a word about what it might have been. Molly hadn't been able to get anything out of him, but maybe I'd have more luck this morning. He'd had some time to think about it, so maybe I could catch his guard down.

I found the same maid who'd tipped me off to his presence cleaning Barry Hill's room as I started to knock on his door.

"Good morning," I said. "Do you have any idea where Mr. Hill is?"

"He's gone," she said. "I'm sorry you missed him."

"Do you have any idea when he's coming back?" I needed to speak with him, and this particular maid had proved to be resourceful in the past.

"No, you don't understand. When I say he's gone, I mean he's gone. He checked out early this morning."

"Blast it all," I said. "I need to find out where he went."

"Max won't tell you," she said as I raced for the door. "So it won't even do you any good to try. He acts like he owns this place, and all of our guests are his family."

"I get it," I said, reaching into my wallet for a twenty.

"I don't want your money," she said. "Not that I wouldn't take it if I had some information for you, but I honestly don't know where the man went."

"Sorry," I said, as I put my wallet back in my pocket.

She accepted the apology with a smile. "You don't have to apologize to me, but you should know that I won't cheat you by lying to you. That's where I draw the line."

"Thanks," I said as I left. "I appreciate that."

We all have our own levels of how far we'll go, where we'll draw the line and say, "there and no more." I could accept the maid's rationalization, mostly because I knew that I made them myself from time to time.

I called Molly, though I wasn't happy about the prospect of talking to her.

When she finally picked up, I said, "Barry Hill checked out early this morning, and no one knows where he's gone."

"Ben, do you make soap at all anymore, or are you too busy playing detective?"

"I try to fit them both in whenever I can," I said, a little harsher than I should have. "I just thought you'd like to know that one of your suspects was taking off." Then, without giving her the chance to say another word, I hung up on her. I'd taken enough guff that morning, and I wasn't in the mood to take any more.

My phone rang twenty seconds later, and I considered not answering it, but then I realized that would be a childish reaction, and I decided to pick up anyway.

"Okay, I'm sorry. I was out of line just then."

I couldn't believe it. Molly actually sounded contrite. "I'm the one who should apologize. I had a fight with Diana and her family earlier, and it shook me up more than I'd like to admit."

"What happened?" she asked.

"I didn't mean to, but before I left their house, I ended up accusing all three of them of murder," I said, then hastily corrected, "No, it wasn't as bad as that. All I really did was ask them for their alibis, but you'd think I'd done a lot worse by the way they reacted."

"I already talked to the Longs," Molly said. "They were in Charlotte for a doctor's appointment with a specialist. It checked out."

"Information I could have used before I said anything," I admitted. "Sorry, I know you aren't under any obligation to keep me in the loop. Is there any chance you've cleared Diana, too?"

"No such luck," she said, "and if you tell anybody I said one word to you about this case, I'll deny it and call you a liar."

"I completely understand," I said. "And in the spirit of

you not telling me anything, were you able to find out what Sharon was doing when Connie Brown was getting murdered at my shop?"

"She claims she overslept, but when Jean tried to get into her room to clean, she said the door was locked. No one saw her as she left the bed-and-breakfast to head over to the soap shop, at least we haven't found any witnesses yet. It's the best we've been able to come up with."

"What about Barry? Does he have an alibi you can check out?" I wasn't at all certain how long Molly would be in the mood to share, but I was going to wring every ounce of information out of her I could in the meantime.

"He claims he was walking aimlessly around town, but again, I haven't found anybody yet who is willing to swear that they saw him." She hesitated, then added, "I looked into Brian Ross's log for that day, because I knew you'd want to know. He was actually writing a parking ticket across town at the time of the murder, but there's something odd about it."

"What's that?"

"Somebody wrote over the time entry on the ticket. He claims he made a mistake and corrected it, but I'm going to look at the ticket and see if the numbers match, or if Ross changed it after the fact."

"Thanks for that," I said. "I appreciate you keeping your options open."

"Until I can prove who killed your contessa, everyone's a suspect."

"In the first place," I said, "she's not my contessa."

"I don't want to hear the other places, thank you very much. Listen, I've got to go, Ben. I'll talk to you later. And don't worry about Barry Hill. He can't go far. We'll find him soon enough."

"I hope you're right."

"Have faith in me and my fellow officers," Molly said, and then she hung up.

I hoped she was right. By fleeing town, Barry Hill was admitting to the world that he was either guilty of murder, or afraid that he might be the next victim.

But which was it?

Twelve

∘ ∘ ∘

I decided I wasn't ready to go back to Where There's Soap just yet, so I drove out to the Mountain Lake Motel to see what Sharon thought about Barry Hill running away. Maybe I could get something else out of her.

I had to knock on the door three times before I got any response, and I was beginning to believe that there had been a mass exodus of suspects from Harper's Landing.

When she finally opened the door, I was more than a little relieved that she was still in town.

When she saw me, Sharon said, "Hi, Ben. Come on in. Sorry it took me so long to answer the door, but I was just on the phone. It turns out my stipend isn't going to last as long as I'd hoped it would. Connie's business manager told me I could stay here one more night, and then I was going to have to finance it myself if I wanted to hang around Harper's Landing. There's some good news, though. He wants me back at Connie's so I can help him sort through her papers, and he's going to pay me while I'm doing it. Connie was a terrible record keeper, and it's going to take forever to sort the mess out, so I don't have to worry about running out and finding a job anytime soon. I'm sorry I can't stay longer."

"You won't be the first one to leave," I said.

"What are you talking about?"

"Barry Hill left this morning. I was wondering if he might have stopped by here on his way out of town."

"No, he didn't come by," she said. "I can't believe the police would just let him leave like that."

"They didn't have anything on him," I said. "Are you sure you don't want to tell me what happened last night? It was pretty obvious you two were arguing about something."

"I don't want to talk about it," she said simply.

I wasn't about to let her off that easy, but there was something else I wanted to ask her first before I managed to alienate her, too, along with every other suspect I was considering. "Sharon, I'd like to talk to you about the day Connie was killed."

"Ben, I've already been over this with the police. I overslept, and that's something I never do." She bit her lower lip, then said, "You know what? I think it might not have been an accident that I missed the signing."

"What are you talking about?"

"The night before Connie was murdered, I was with her in her room. She told me she wanted some rest time by herself, and I understood, since we'd been working hard on her next book. Anyway, when I got back to my room, a few things were out of place, and my bottled water wasn't exactly where I'd left it. Is it possible that someone drugged my drink so I would be absent the next day at the signing?"

"Why would someone want you out of the picture?" I asked.

"Connie demanded constant attention whenever she appeared in public. If the killer was planning to get rid of her all along at your shop, wouldn't it make sense to get me out of the way first?"

I would be the first to admit that Connie Brown had been demanding the day of the signing, and I wasn't even one of her employees. It wasn't that big a stretch to believe that she'd have had Sharon jumping through hoops to have everything just so. "But who could have done it?"

"I know you're not going to like to hear this, but Diana was at the bed-and-breakfast that night."

"Don't forget, so were Brian Ross and Barry Hill."

"True. The only suspect it rules out is Betsy Blair. Unless she slipped in without me seeing her, I doubt she could have done that."

"But neither one of us can say for sure, can we? There's just too much I don't know right now," I said.

Sharon nodded. "Don't beat yourself up about it, Ben. From the way Molly was talking, she's not any closer to figuring out who killed Connie than you are, and she's a professional."

"That's because we don't have all the facts," I said. "If you'd tell her why you were fighting with Barry Hill, maybe it would help."

She bit her lower lip, then said, "What can it hurt now? You were right. He was threatening me."

"About what?"

"I saw him when I came to the signing late. He was loitering near the edge of your shop, and he told me if I told anybody else that I'd seen him there, he'd make me regret it."

"He's already admitted to the police that he was walking around town," I said.

"Yes, but did he confess that he was hovering near your shop? That's not all. When I saw him, I noticed that there was something on his shirt when I ran into him. I'm no expert, but it looked like there were a few flecks of blood on it."

"That might have been helpful to know when he was still around," I said angrily.

"He threatened me," Sharon whined. "What could I do?"

"Hang on one second," I said. "I need to make a call."

"What are you going to do? You said it yourself. Barry's already gone."

"Molly's got the state police out looking for him," I said. "She needs to hear this."

I couldn't get a signal on my cell phone in the room. "I need to step outside to make this call."

"I'll be right here."

I called Molly and told her what I'd just heard. She didn't sound all that surprised as she said, "That's just one more thing I can ask him, if he ever turns up."

"I figured he'd be easy to snag," I said.

"So did I. I'm still not sure how he's managing it, but so far, nobody's laid eyes on him."

I knocked on the door again, and saw that Sharon was packing. "I thought you had one more day," I said as I saw her stuff a blue dress, two pairs of jeans, a crimson hat, more frilly undergarments than one woman should need on a proposed three-day stay, and a paisley scarf into her bag.

"I do," she said, "but I'm getting antsy just sitting here in this room. I've got to get back to Connie's place. There's so much work that needs to be done."

"I understand," I said. "But do me one favor. Call me before you leave, okay?"

"I will," she said as she continued to stuff things into her bag.

"Speaking of bags, you left Connie's at the bed-and-breakfast. I suppose you'll be wanting them, won't you?"

"You can give them to charity for all I care," she said.

"Fine, I'll take care of it."

She hesitated, then said, "On second thought, I'd better take them back with me. Do you have them in your car?"

The bags in question were indeed currently in my trunk, but I wasn't ready to admit that. If I could keep Sharon in town a little longer, she might just help solve the case. I had a feeling the woman knew more than she even realized. "I'll have to bring them by later."

"If you don't have time, I'll pick them up on my way out of town," she said. "Sorry I held back on you before."

"You were frightened," I said. "It's easy enough to understand. Was that it, though?"

She looked confused by the question. "What do you mean?"

"Is there anything, anything at all, that you might not be telling us? Even if it doesn't seem all that important, you need to tell me everything."

She looked as though she was ready to cry. "I've told you all I know." As she sniffed into a tissue, she asked, "Was Molly mad?"

"With her, it's hard to tell lately. Sharon, be careful while you're here, okay?"

"Who would want to hurt me, Ben? I didn't see anything, I wasn't even around when Connie was murdered, and I barely have two dimes to my name."

"You saw Barry with blood on his shirt," I said solemnly. "That might be enough."

"I'll be careful," she said.

I drove back to the soap shop, wondering if there could be anything in Connie's suitcase or garment bag that might give me some idea who had murdered her. Molly had already looked through them, and I probably wouldn't have any more luck than she had in her search, but I had the time, and it wasn't like many more leads were raining down on me. I snuck in the back way at the soap shop, barely acknowledged my brothers with a slight wave, then hurried upstairs before someone could ask me if I was going on a trip.

My desk was covered with paperwork, so I used my grandfather's work space. He hadn't used it in ages, and there was a thin layer of dust on top of it.

I opened Connie's luggage and started digging through the two pieces, but that wasn't getting me anywhere. I finally decided to put them on the floor and pull each item out and look at it as I went. Her lingerie, and she had a lot of it, must have been expensive, based on the diaphanous nature of her collection. I felt really strange going through her delicates. At least there weren't places anything could be concealed, whether while being worn or not.

I looked in the garment bag, knowing that Connie—in her guise as the contessa—would require more formal wear. There were dresses, soft-brimmed hats, and shoes in the pouches, but nothing that looked like it didn't belong. I smiled when I realized that she had complete outfits in blue and green, from the shoes to the dresses and gloves to the floppy hats.

As I suspected, there were no blue jeans in either bag,

no comfortable clothes at all except a bathrobe that looked well worn. I was about ready to give up on that when I noticed that there was a makeup bag buried within the folds of the robe. I decided that, since I was searching, I'd do a thorough job of it, but if there was something there that was out of place, it was beyond my scope of knowledge to figure it out. I packed everything back up and wondered what I had missed. Something nagged at the back of my mind, but I couldn't put my finger on it, and the harder I tried, the less chance I had of capturing it. It would come to me eventually—I knew that from past experience—and there was nothing I could do to rush it.

In the meantime, I still had a murder to solve.

There was a knock on the door, though it was Paulus's office, not mine.

"Come in," I said as I latched the suitcase shut and put it down beside the garment bag.

"Oh, it's you, Benjamin," Mom said as she came into the room. "I was wondering if your grandfather came back early from Europe and neglected to tell anyone of his arrival."

"I needed some space."

"Have you uncovered anything yet?"

"That's the problem. I've got reasons each of my suspects could have done it. Instead of narrowing the field, I'm expanding it. At the rate I'm going, I'll have all of Harper's Landing in my sights before long."

She patted my shoulder. "You'll do it, Benjamin, I have faith in you." She gestured to the luggage. "Are you going somewhere?"

"These are Connie's things. Sharon left them at Jean's bed-and-breakfast, and I promised to get them to her before she goes."

"So you thought the most direct route was through this office?"

I couldn't exactly deny what I'd been doing. "I admit it. I got nosy and started snooping."

"It's not being nosy, you're being productive. So, what did you find?"

"I learned that Connie hated blue jeans, but loved to co-ordinate her outfits from top to bottom."

Mom nodded. "She liked to play the role of diva, didn't she? You must remember, though, she may have done some bad things in her life, but she was still a soapmaker at heart."

"Is that supposed to absolve her of everything else, just because she shared our vocation?"

"Benjamin, you know better than that. Keep digging. I believe you will uncover the truth."

"I'm glad one of us does," I said. "Walk back to my office with me. I want to show you something."

"Certainly," she said, then gestured to the suitcases. "What are you going to do with those?"

"Let's just leave them here for now," I said. "I'll give them to Sharon when she comes by later. She's leaving town, and Barry Hill is already gone. I'm beginning to wonder if we'll ever solve this while our suspects are still around."

"What does Molly think?" Mom asked as she closed the door behind us and started toward my office.

"Honestly? I think she believes Diana did it. I'd be lying if I said she didn't have enough reason to want to see the woman dead. Connie Brown stole her mother and father from her, and there's a hatred burning inside Diana that was a little frightening to see."

"She's lost a great deal," Mom said. "She's allowed to be angry."

"I guess so," I said as I opened my office door and led Mom inside. "She also stands to inherit a hundred thousand dollars from Connie's estate, though I'm not supposed to tell anyone that, and I'd appreciate it if you'd keep it a secret, too."

"You know you can trust me to watch what I say, Benjamin."

I nodded. "I don't like what this has been doing to Diana and me—investigating this murder is driving a wedge between us that we may not be able to fix once it's all over."

"You've got to have faith that things will work out for the best," she said. "Now what is it you'd like me to see in here?" She looked around the room, then added, "I can see you're not showing off your organizational skills. This place is an absolute wreck, Benjamin."

"Hey, that's not fair. I have a system. I can find whatever I'm looking for. Now where did I put that envelope I wanted to show you?"

She was about to crow about my statement when she saw my grin. "Benjamin, if I haven't told you lately, you're incorrigible."

"Thanks, it's important to be good at something." I retrieved the photographs that Rufus had given me and searched through the pile for the one I wanted.

"Look at this," I said as I held the picture out to her. It was a shot of the place before anyone else was there, and Where There's Soap looked warm and inviting, in stark contrast to the shot the newspaper had run. "I thought we might be able to use this on our next brochure."

She studied the print, then asked, "Did you take this yourself?"

"No, Diana's clerk, Rufus, did. It's good, isn't it?"

"I like it," she said. "Let's buy it from him."

"I'm sure he'd be happy to just give it to us," I said.

"Nonsense. It would cost us good money if a professional photographer took this. If we're going to use it for our business, we need to show payment and that the rights have been assigned to us. You should go make him an offer for the negative and all publishing rights. Make him sign a release, too."

"How much should I give him? Would a hundred dollars be too much?"

Mom's eyes grew large. "Not unless you're going to match what the shop is willing to pay. Give him fifty. He'll be glad to get it, I wager."

"Okay, I'll take care of it later."

"Ben, you should do it now."

I didn't really want to go to the bookstore, but then I realized that there was no danger of running into Diana there. She was in Hunter's Hollow with her aunt and uncle, so now would be a perfect time to do it. "Let me print out a release and I'll be on my way. Would you mind cutting me a check while I do this?"

"I'd be happy to."

She left to draw a check on the company account, and I printed a copy of the standard release form we used. It was easy enough to fill in the blanks with Rufus's name and the amount, and by the time I had it ready, Mom was back with a check.

"What about these photographs?" Mom asked. "Aren't you going to take them back to him?"

"No, he gave them to me outright."

"You're at least going to put them away before you go, aren't you?" she asked.

"No, I'm not finished with them. I'll get them later."

I took off, grabbing the photo in question so Rufus could retrieve the negative. There was no doubt in my mind he would have signed the rights over to me for nothing, but I didn't want to take advantage of him that way. Besides, I figured he'd be thrilled to make his first professional sale.

I was wrong.

"RUFUS, I can't believe you're being so stubborn. I thought you'd be delighted to make your first sale."

He shrugged. "I'm not surprised you think so. That's not the way I operate, though. I take photographs as a hobby. I'm not trying to generate an income here. Just take it. I don't care. Here's the negative, too. If I want another one, I'll snap the photo myself."

"I can't go back without this release signed," I said. "And that means you have to take the check, too."

"Then you can't have it," he said. "I'm an artist, Ben. I don't sell things, but that doesn't keep me from giving them away."

He was driving me nuts, but at least there wasn't anybody around to witness the exchange. Not only was Diana absent from the store, so were all of their customers. Was the thrill they'd experienced knowing a murder suspect gone now that the reality of the situation was starting to sink in?

"Okay, if you won't take the money, how about if I buy you fifty dollars worth of books?"

He sneered at me. "Why would I want you to do that? I can read anything I want behind the counter, and when I'm finished with it, I just put it back on the shelf."

"Would you be interested in a gift certificate to the soap

shop?" I asked, desperate to come up with anything valued at fifty dollars so the books would be balanced.

"Thanks, but no, I don't think so."

What was I going to do to get him to take payment for his work? "You could use it for photographic supplies. I know you're getting a great rate on your prints, but they've got to be costing you something."

"I don't know," he said, but I could see that he was starting to waver.

"You know what?" I said. "I apologize. I've been approaching this all wrong. What I meant to say when I walked in just now was that I'd like to contribute to the further development of your art, since you so generously donated a photograph to my business. Don't look at me that way, the government gives grants all the time for developing artists. You've heard of the National Endowment for the Arts, haven't you?"

"Sure," Rufus said.

"Then consider this the Harper's Landing Endowment Society."

"There's no such thing," he said.

I handed him the check. "There is now, and you're our first recipient. Congratulations."

"Cool," he said as he finally took the check.

"Just sign here and we'll be finished."

"I'm not selling the picture, Ben, I told you."

I nodded. "You don't have to." I took the form from him, crossed out the fifty and wrote one, then handed it back to him. "Sign now."

"It doesn't matter whether it's a buck or a million, it's the principle."

"Consider the dollar as part of your endowment then."

He thought about that for nearly a minute, then said, "I can live with that."

I had the signed paper, the negative, and the print, and Rufus had a check for fifty dollars, plus a single out of my own wallet. It had been way too much work completing the transaction, but in the end, everyone's sensibilities had been met.

I started for the door when Rufus said, "Hang on a second."

I waited while he dug through a pile of photographs on the counter. "I almost forgot. Here are the rest of the shots I took of your shop."

"I thought you already gave them all to me."

"No, this was from the roll still in my camera."

I knew what the answer was going to be, but I had to ask anyway. "Can I pay you for these?"

"Not a chance," he said with a grin as he held up my check. "I've got it covered. I just got an endowment."

I laughed as I left, happy that at least one thing had gone right today. I took the new photographs and put them on the Miata's passenger seat. I was about to drive off when I heard someone calling my name. It was Kelly Sheer, and from the expression on her face, something was terribly wrong.

Thirteen

○ ○ ○

"**Ben,** do you have a second?" she asked, looking into the bookstore as she said it. "I won't take much of your time. I'm sure you're busy."

"Actually, I'm not," I said. I noticed that Kelly was still staring inside Dying To Read. "You don't have to worry. She's not in there."

"It doesn't matter anymore, does it?" she said. "Would you mind coming over to my office? I'd be more comfortable talking to you there."

We both noticed Rufus watching us, and I said, "That sounds like a good idea. Let me move my car, and I'll meet you over there."

I saluted Rufus, then got into the Miata. It was a quicker walk than it was a drive, since I had to go around the block to find a spot, but the last thing in the world I wanted was for Diana to come back and spot my car parked in front of her bookstore.

Kelly was waiting for me as I pulled up in front of her office. "I appreciate you doing this, Ben."

"I'm happy to," I said, though I was dying of curiosity about why she wanted to talk to me.

I was surprised to find boxes in Kelly's outer office.

"What's going on?" I asked as I followed her in. "Are you getting a partner?"

"No, it's nothing like that," she said. "Ben, there's no easy way to say this, so I'll just tell you straight out. I'm leaving Harper's Landing."

"Why?" I was honestly shocked. When Kelly had moved to town, I thought she'd be here for good.

I could see she was fighting back tears, but she kept a stoic expression as she said, "This reconciliation with Wade has been a disaster. I probably don't have to tell you that, do I?"

"I knew you were going through a rough patch," I admitted.

"It's been more than that," she said. "We've both finally realized that we just don't make sense together."

"How's Annie taking it?" I asked. Kelly's daughter had been a big reason we'd had so much trouble, but I'd never blamed her for a second. What child of divorced parents didn't want them to get back together at some point in their lives?

"Do you want to know the truth? I think she's relieved."

"Then it's probably for the best. I don't understand why you have to move away from Harper's Landing, though. We're going to miss you."

Kelly bit her lip for a second, then said, "Wade's going back to Charlotte, and though he probably doesn't care if he ever sees me again, he finally realizes how much he's missed Annie. She's bonded with him too since he's been here, and I can't keep them apart."

I stood. "Kelly, I can't tell you how to run your life, but you've got a stake in this, too."

"What do you mean?"

I was trying to keep my anger inside, but I wasn't doing a very good job of it. "Charlotte's just an hour and half away. Let him come up whenever he wants to see her, but don't give up your new life here, your new friends."

She shook her head. "It's not that simple."

"It can be if you want it to be," I said.

"I'm sorry, Ben."

"I am, too." I left, afraid of what else I might say. It wasn't the way I would have preferred to say good-bye, but then I didn't think she should go. Sacrificing for her child was one thing, but she was doing this for the convenience of her ex-husband, a man who didn't deserve the consideration, from everything she'd told me about him. Nothing I'd seen or heard around town had contradicted my low opinion of the man, either.

I drove back to the soap shop, more miserable than I'd been in quite awhile. A few days ago, I'd been happy being with Diana and was just starting to get used to having Kelly as a friend. Now it looked like neither one of them would be in my life very much longer. Though Diana wasn't moving away—at least not that I knew of—she'd moved away from me in her heart. Honestly, the damage that had been done recently might never be repaired.

I barely said a word to my brothers and sisters as I stormed up to my office. In a fit of anger, I brushed my desk clear with the back of one arm, sending bills, invoices, and Rufus's photographs flying through the room.

Mom picked that moment to come in without knocking.

"Benjamin," she said as she studied the mess on the floor, "if you'd planned to redecorate in here, the least you could have done was tell me about it beforehand."

As I started to clean up the mess, she bent down to help.

"I've got it," I said, not meaning to snap at her, but not able to pull it back in, either.

"Nonsense. Do you expect me to stand here and watch you work? It will go faster if we work together."

"Suit yourself," I said.

As we sorted the photographs from the rest of the papers, Mom said, "I know there must be some reason for this outburst."

"There is," I said.

She stared at me a moment, then asked, "Would you care to share it with your mother?"

"Not particularly."

"How about one of your brothers or sisters? They're all concerned about you, Benjamin."

I shook my head. "Well, tell them not to worry. I'm just peachy keen."

"I can see that," she said, raising one eyebrow as she did.

Finally, I couldn't take it anymore. "Kelly's leaving town," I announced, "and the way Diana and I are going, we won't be together much longer either."

Mom took it in and continued to work.

Finally, she said, "And which event bothers you more?"

"That's an excellent question," I said. "And I wish I had an excellent answer for you. Honestly, the truth is, I don't know."

"Thus the explosion," she said. "As tantrums go, this wasn't much of one, was it?"

I smiled at her. "Would it make you feel better if I threw my chair through the window?"

"No, I think you contained yourself rather well, given the circumstances. How odd."

I didn't even look up as I kept working. "What, that I managed to keep my temper in check?"

I looked over at her and saw that she was staring at a photograph. "This wasn't here before."

I looked at what she was holding and saw another image of the soap shop, this one with a crowd of people standing around waiting to get in. "So? Rufus gave me the rest of his prints. He was pleased we liked his work." There was no need to go into detail on the tap dance I'd had to do to get him to accept our money.

Mom tapped the picture with her index finger. "Benjamin, do you see this?"

I took it from her and studied it. There was a woman wearing a red hat a few steps away from the crowd, and though most of her body was obscured by the camera lens, the hat was clear enough. "What about it?"

"It's the same hat as the one in Connie Brown's publicity photo. So why wasn't she wearing it when she came into the shop?"

"Who knows," I said. "Maybe she got tired of it." I looked a little harder at the picture and saw someone else I hadn't noticed in any of the shots before. Brian Ross, the cop who had come up with an alibi across town when the Soap Celebration was going on, was standing in front of Where There's Soap. There was something about his body language that made me think he was coiled and ready to strike. Though his back was turned to the contessa, I couldn't help wondering if he'd been there to deal with her rejection of him.

"Spread out the photographs so we can see if there's one before or after this one," I commanded. "We need to see if Rufus took any of these in sequence."

Mom and I gathered all of the shots together and laid them on my clean desktop, but the one she'd spotted was the only image that showed either figure in it.

Mom said, "Call Rufus and see if he took any more pictures."

"We've got them all," I said. "This is the only one that shows either one of them."

I grabbed the picture and started for the door. "Where are you going, Benjamin? And what about this mess?"

"Leave it," I said. "I need to talk to Molly."

I went to the police station and found the same gruff desk sergeant there who had given me a hard time before.

"I need to see Detective Wilkes," I said.

"Sorry, she's unavailable," he said, barely looking up from his paperwork.

"Can you tell me where she is?"

"No," he said as he looked up at me, then added, "department policy."

I walked outside and called her on my cell phone. When she picked up, I said, "Molly, I need to see you, but the pit bull at the front desk won't let me in."

"Ben, I really don't have time for you right now."

"You'll want to see what I've got in my hand. Believe me."

She hesitated, then said, "Go wait in your car. I'll be out in ten minutes."

I did as I was told, and the more I stared at the photograph, the more convinced I was that Brian Ross was at our shop for all the wrong reasons. There was something about the man that set me on edge. I just hoped Molly could see it.

There was a tap on my window fifteen minutes later, and Molly got in the passenger seat of the Miata. "What's so important?"

I handed her the photograph. "Recognize anyone?"

She studied it for a few seconds, then said, "It's Brian Ross."

"I thought he was somewhere else during the event at my shop."

"So did I," she said.

"There's something else. See that woman in the red hat?"

"Barely," Molly acknowledged.

"It's Connie Brown. Don't you find it more than a little odd that he's that close to her? Look at the way he's standing. It shouts out that he's angry about something."

"Ben, in the first place, I have no idea if that's Connie Brown in the hat. You could barely prove that it's a woman to me from that angle. Can you honestly say it's her under that trench coat? As for Ross, I'll talk to him as soon as he gets back. I'm sure we'll be able to clear up the reason he was there."

"Where did he go?"

"Don't read anything into this, but he took his vacation time, starting this morning. He'll be back in two weeks."

"Don't you see? He's running away."

She shook her head. "I don't think so. Believe me, when he gets back, I'll ask him about this."

"Have you had any luck finding Barry Hill?"

"No," she admitted reluctantly. "I don't get it. It's like he just vanished."

"I'm beginning to wonder if he'll ever turn up," I said.

She stared at me. "Ben, what are you talking about?"

"He was Ross's biggest rival for Connie's affections. If

your cop killed her first, why wouldn't he go after Hill next?"

"You've been reading too many of your girlfriend's detective novels," Molly said.

"I haven't, and besides, I don't think she's my girlfriend anymore." It sounded awkward as I said it, and I almost wished I hadn't.

"What happened?" There was no harshness in Molly's voice as she asked.

"This murder got in the way," I said. "Did you hear the other news? Kelly Sheer's moving to Charlotte."

Molly nodded. "I just heard myself. If this keeps up, there won't be a woman left in town who's willing to go out with you."

"Quite a track record, isn't it? You're not going anywhere, are you?"

She waited so long to say something that I thought she might be leaving, too. I didn't know if I could take it. Finally, she said, "I'm still going to work here, but I guess in a way I'm leaving you, too. Jeff asked me to marry him, and I said yes."

"What?" I asked, rubbing my forehead. "Are you kidding me?"

She shook her head. "I didn't want to tell you this way, but you need to know so you can have time to deal with it. We're telling your family tomorrow night, so act surprised, okay?"

I thought of a thousand things I could say, but the only thing that was appropriate was the one I finally chose. "Congratulations."

"Ben, do you mean that?"

"I wish you both the best," I said. "Molly, we knew a long time ago that we were better friends than lovers. If you can find happiness with my little brother, then I'm truly glad for you."

Molly kissed my cheek. "Jeff's going to be so relieved. He's been scared to death ever since I said yes."

"Do you have to tell him my reaction right away?" I asked. "At least give me another day to make his life a little miserable. I've got just the idea. I'm going over to his place tonight and tell him he's got to give you up, that I can't bear the thought of living without you another day."

She laughed at the image. "You're wicked, you know that, don't you?"

"Thanks, coming from you, that's really special. So, will you let me have a little fun before I give him my blessing?"

"Sorry," she said, smiling to prove that she wasn't sorry at all. "If he's going to be my husband, I'm not going to keep any secrets from him."

"Hey, you're not even married yet."

"Ben, don't even try it. I'm calling him the second you pull out."

"Spoilsport," I said. "Seriously, I'm happy for you both."

"Thanks." She opened the car door, then tapped the photograph. "Can I hang on to this?"

"Sure. If I need another copy, I'll get Rufus to make one for me."

"Now why on earth would you need another copy?" she asked me.

"Just because you're joining our family doesn't mean I'm going to stop snooping. You knew that, didn't you?"

"As much as I'd hoped otherwise, I guess I did."

I drove off, wondering what to make of what my life had become. The three women in the world I cared about that weren't relatives were all leaving me, one way or another. I was so stunned by what had happened, it had barely had time to sink in yet.

I'd have to worry about that later, though. The best way for me to get over the shocks I'd just had at the moment was to help Molly find Connie Brown's killer, whether she wanted my assistance or not.

My suspects were leaving town faster than I could deal with them. Betsy Blair was gone. Brian Ross was on vacation. Who knew where Barry Hill had disappeared to, or if he was even still alive? Diana was at her aunt and uncle's house, and Sharon Goldsmith was leaving as fast as she could get out of Harper's Landing. Connie Brown's murder was in serious danger of slipping into the open but unsolved files of the Harper's Landing police department.

As cold as it may have sounded, I wasn't just trying to solve the homicide for her sake. Our business was dying at the soap shop, and if the rumors and stories about us kept up, we might be another casualty of the crime. While I couldn't bring Connie back, I had to save my family's business if I could. It was all I had left in the world.

I decided to talk to Sharon while she was still in town, but I wanted another copy of that photograph before I spoke with her. It meant another trip to Dying To Read, but I was hoping Diana was still out of town.

Unfortunately, she wasn't.

"Ben, I'm through talking to you. I thought I made that clear," Diana said as I walked into the store.

"I'm not here to see you," I said. "I want to talk to Rufus."

"Too bad, you're out of luck. I sent him home. He's

been working so much overtime lately, I can barely afford to pay him as it is. My customers have deserted me completely."

"It's bad at the soap shop, too."

"At least no one's accused you of murder," she snapped.

"Not lately, anyway." A thought occurred to me. "You shouldn't have to worry about your cash flow, not for a while."

"What are you talking about?" She honestly had no idea what I was talking about, and I realized I wasn't supposed to tell her about the inheritance.

"Nothing, I misspoke," I said.

"Ben, tell me."

There was no way out of it now. I'd have to apologize to Sharon later if it came up. "Connie left you one hundred thousand dollars in her will."

Diana flew into a rage. "Did she honestly think she could buy me off with money? I won't take it. I don't want it. It's blood money."

"Give it to charity, then."

Her anger blazed directly at me. "Get out, Ben."

"I'm going," I said.

If she could have slammed the door behind me, there was no doubt in my mind that she would have.

I had nowhere else to go, so I decided to talk to my last suspect. I just hoped Sharon hadn't left yet.

As I drove to the Mountain Lake Motel, I noticed that a nondescript white Chevy was following me. I never would have noticed it under normal circumstances, but I decided to get a pack of gum and pulled into Crites Drugs at the last second. The car passed by me, but the driver obscured his face as he came even with me—dodging behind a folded newspaper—just enough to block my view of him. I bought the gum, got back into the Miata, and drove to the motel. Two miles up the road, I noticed that the Chevy was back. What was going on? I decided to go on ahead to Sharon's room and call Molly from there. I wanted to make sure I wasn't just being paranoid before I brought her into it.

"Ben, what are you doing here?" Sharon asked as she opened her door. "I was just leaving."

"I'm glad I caught you," I said, looking over my shoulder. The Chevy was gone, but that didn't mean it wouldn't be back. "I was afraid you'd already be gone."

"I would have been, but there was a problem with my credit card," she admitted. "I've been waiting for Connie's executor to pay for the room with his own plastic, and I just got confirmation that he has, so I'm leaving right now."

"Are you sure you can't hang around one more day? We'll pick up the tab for the room if you'll stay."

"I told you I was needed back at Connie's place. Besides, I couldn't stomach the thought of staying in this town one more night." She waved a hand around the room. "I mean seriously, can you blame me?"

"Can I at least have a second?" I asked. "There's something I want to talk to you about."

She frowned, glanced at her watch, then stepped aside. "You can have five minutes, but then I'm leaving."

I stepped inside, then pulled the drapes away from the window and looked outside. The Chevy was nowhere in sight.

"What are you looking at?"

"It's probably just my imagination," I said.

"So what do you want to talk about?" she asked.

"There's a photograph you should see, but the only problem is, I gave my only copy to the police, and I haven't had a chance to get another one made yet."

"So?"

"It's of the soap shop on the day of the signing," I explained.

That got her interest. "I didn't realize you were having the event photographed."

"I didn't, but a friend of mine thought it would be a good idea. He didn't take any close-ups, though. All of the shots were outside. One of them in particular caught my eye."

"Go on," she said. "You don't mind if I finish packing while you talk, do you? As fascinating as your story is, I still plan to leave as soon as possible."

"That's fine," I said, realizing that I was losing her attention. "There's a shot of a woman out front in a red hat like Connie usually wore," I said, "And there's another man nearby, Brian Ross. You remember him, don't you?"

She turned toward me, and it took me a second to realize there was a gun in her hand.

"What are you doing?"

"What does it look like? Who has the photograph? And who took it? I'm going to need that negative before I go."

Then it all clicked. "That was you in the hat, wasn't it? I even saw you pack it in your bag. You weren't drugged at all. Did you use it as a disguise so you could kill Connie? Why?"

"Have you ever noticed what great camouflage those floppy hats make? Connie was furious when hers was missing, but I was hoping if anyone saw me, they'd mistake me for her. After all, she was wearing it during all of the publicity shots you used, I made sure of that. It would have worked, too, if you hadn't had a photographer snooping around."

"But why kill her?" I asked.

"Why else? Greed."

That didn't make any sense. "You said Diana got the bulk of her estate. I thought you claimed you just got a token amount."

"It wasn't the money I was after, it was the copyrights. She willed them to me, the silly cow. When she found out I'd been dipping into her bank accounts, she was going to fire me and change her will, so I decided to take matters into my own hands. You didn't know it was me until just a second ago, did you?"

"I didn't have a clue," I admitted. "But it all makes sense now. I still don't know why you killed her in my family's shop."

"Think about it. You're a smart guy. If I'd killed her in her room at the bed-and-breakfast, everyone would look at me as a major suspect. As it was, there was a whole mob of people who wanted her dead, and they all had access to the crime scene. I made sure of that by leaving the back door open. I was going to shoot her," she added, "but there were too many people around. The hammer did the job just as nicely, and it was much quieter, too."

"You're never going to get away with this," I said.

"Oh, poor naive Ben," she said. "As far as I'm concerned, I already have. Now it's just a matter of tying up a few loose ends, and you're the next one on my list."

"Did you kill Barry Hill, too?" I asked, hoping to buy some time.

She appeared to be absolutely delighted by the concept. When she stopped laughing, she explained, "No, he's alive, at least as far as I know; but I did give him a reason to run. You see, I told him if he didn't leave town immediately, I'd tell the police about how he'd blackmailed money out of Connie. He did, you know. Those lurid photographs wouldn't help his image any, but they would have destroyed Connie's career. She had a wholesome image to protect as an author of soap-crafting books, and she was willing to pay to keep it. Your little girlfriend wasn't the only person Connie tried to pay off. She was hoping that if she could silence Barry Hill with money, no one would ever have to know what a bad little girl she'd been. He claims to be rich, but he had less than I do. I had hoped Barry would die in a shoot-out with the police, but I'm afraid they haven't been able to find him."

"What about Betsy Blair? Did Connie steal the book from her?"

Sharon shook her head. "Believe it or not, the contessa was actually innocent of that particular crime. The woman fabricated a new copy of 'her' book and was trying to use it to get Connie to settle out of court. She didn't have a prayer, and neither do you. I'm afraid you're the one who's going to have to pay for that photographer's mistake."

I had to do something quick or I was going to be dead. "Molly Wilkes and Brian Ross both know I'm here."

She laughed. "Ben, you're a terrible liar. If I'd just waited to hear what you had to say, I wouldn't have to kill you right now. Sorry about that. I guess I jumped the gun, and now you have to face one."

The door behind me crashed open, and Brian Ross knocked me to the ground just as Sharon fired in our direction. Ross's gun barked twice, and Sharon crumpled to the floor.

"Are you all right?" I asked him, still staring at Sharon's lifeless body.

"No, she hit me. Call an ambulance, will you?"

I dialed 911, and as soon as I hung up, I said, "That was you in the Chevy, wasn't it? Why were you following me?"

He shrugged, and I saw him wince from the pain. "You were the wild card in all of this. I figured you had a good shot at figuring out who killed my Connie, and I wanted to be nearby in case you needed backup."

"I'd be dead without you," I said. "I don't know the proper way to thank you for that."

He shook his head. "You've got it all wrong. The way I see it, we're dead even."

"How do you get that?"

"You led me to her," he said. "That balances the books. A lot of folks say they don't believe in an eye for an eye, but I'm not one of them."

"Would you have shot her if she hadn't tried to kill me?" I asked.

He was just getting ready to answer when the ambulance pulled up, and I doubted that I would ever find out.

FOURTEEN

. . .

AS the paramedics loaded Brian Ross onto the cart, a third man checked Sharon briefly, then shook his head and rejoined the others. Molly was there before they could drive off, and I saw her have a few words with him.

After the ambulance was gone, Molly asked me, "Are you all right?"

"The bullet missed me and hit Ross instead," I said.

"That's not what I mean. I'm not talking about bullet wounds."

I shook my head. "Honestly? I don't know. I'm not sure I ever will be." That was true enough. My system had been through so many shocks in the last two hours I wasn't sure I'd ever be able to recover.

"Come on, let's get you out of here."

"Don't you need a statement from me?" I asked as we walked outside.

"Yeah, but we can do it out here just as easily as we can in there."

I was more grateful than I could say to get out of that room. It was almost as if it had happened to someone else, and I'd been watching it on a movie screen. That bullet had come close enough to hitting me instead of Ross that I could have sworn I felt the breeze off it as it passed.

After I brought Molly up to date on what had happened, she asked, "Do you want me to call somebody for you?"

"There's no one to call," I said. "I'm going home."

"I don't think you should be alone right now, Ben," she said.

"That's too bad, because that's exactly where I am in my life," I said.

Over her protests, I got into my Miata and drove toward home, but on a last-second impulse, I headed to Where There's Soap instead. I had to share what had happened with my family. Later, I wanted a hot shower to try to scrub the memory of that attack away, but for now, I needed to be around the people who loved me. I knew there wasn't a soap in the world that could clean the darkness in my heart, but I had to try. I wasn't sure what would happen with my life, but I wasn't going to waste another second of it wishing and hoping for things that weren't ever going to happen. It was time to start living each and every moment I had left. If that brought love in my life, I was ready for it, but if not, that would be fine, too.

I had my family, our business, and my health.

The way I looked at it, everything else was icing.

I was nearly at the back door of the shop when I saw Kelly Sheer approaching me on foot.

I walked back down the stairs and met her in the back parking lot. "What are you doing here?"

She said, "I was in the courthouse talking to a deputy when Molly's call came in. Ben, are you all right?"

"It was close, but she missed me. I'm a little shaky, but I'll be fine."

She looked like she was going to cry again.

"Kelly, are you okay?"

That's when she broke down. "No, I'm not. Ben, I'm miserable. I've made a horrible mistake. I thought I could sacrifice myself for Annie's sake, but I can't. I don't want to leave Harper's Landing." She wiped away her tears, then looked at me with a steady gaze before she said, "Ben, I know I've hurt you deeply, and I realize you're seeing someone else, but I have to ask. Is there any chance for us again?"

I stood there staring at her for nearly a full minute, not knowing what my answer was going to be.

Diana and I were finished, that much was clear. I'd seen the hatred in her eyes when she'd looked at me, and though I could forgive her, I doubted that I'd ever be able to forget how she'd turned on me. There was no going back for us.

But could I start things up with Kelly again? A lot had happened between us, but if I was being true to my heart, I had to acknowledge that I still had strong feelings for her. There was a pull there that I couldn't explain.

"I'd like that," I said.

Before I could finish my sentence, she was in my arms, and I knew I'd made the right decision.

SOAPMAKING TIPS
FOR THE HOME HOBBYIST

o o o

TYPES OF FRAGRANCES USED IN SOAPMAKING

THERE are several types of fragrances that can be used in soapmaking.

Oils, extracts, herbs, and infused oils can all add aroma to your soap. Choosing the right type of fragrance can create a wondrous soap unique to you, or, if you're not careful, it may completely ruin your batch. Fragrance oils should be specifically designed for soapmaking; otherwise, your batch could seize up into a hard rock before it's had a chance to set.

Extracts are not overly strong, so while they can be used, it may take a lot to get the desired fragrance.

Herbs can be a good choice, but they should be dried and ground before using.

Finally, oil infused with flowers from your own aromatic garden can be used, and the result adds a personal touch that can't be replicated by an impersonal production line.

ADDING FRAGRANCES TO YOUR SOAPS, BATH PRODUCTS, LIP BALMS, AND HAND LOTIONS

WHEN adding fragrances to everything from handcrafted soaps to the hand lotions and lip balms mentioned in this book, it's important to remember that a little bit goes a long way. I like to use oils that are already extracted and ready to use. Though they are expensive, I'm sure about the consistent quality of the product.

Some of the more popular scents I like to use in soaps and other personal care products are lavender, sandlewood, peppermint, eucalyptus, and rosemary. When combining more than one scent in a batch, it's important to keep in mind that some scents are complementary, while others clash.

Whenever I create a new scent for a particular soap, I like to start with very small amounts of oil added to cotton swabs, then I move on to a small test batch if I like the result. That way, by using a pipette to add small quantities of essential oils, I can tell if I'm going to like the combination before I commit to making a bigger batch of soap. This is especially important when dealing with a soap that takes a long time to cure, and remember, the oils are expensive, so it's best to test it on a small batch first.

When buying essential oils, or any additive to your soap, it's important to remember that less expensive products may be diluted or are modified with extenders. Many times, you do indeed get what you pay for.

Scents can add a wonderful dimension to your handcrafted soaps, so don't be afraid to experiment. Some of the combinations that have been popular in the past include lavender and rosemary, cinnamon and orange, and rosemary, sage, and thyme. Have fun!

OTHER SOAPMAKING ADDITIVES

NOT all soap additives have to be fragrant. There are many choices in dyes you can use to make your soap unique, and there are also natural elements that make your creations all yours.

Oatmeal is a popular additive, used to soothe sensitive or irritated skin. Use rolled or long-cooking oats for your batch, though. Quick cook or instant oatmeal may thicken your soap before it has the chance to set, making it impossible to mold.

Dried luffa gourds make wonderful containers for your homemade soap. Wrap a luffa in plastic wrap, then pour your soap into the center. It makes a wonderful present, too, since the presentation is so interesting.

GET CLUED IN

Ever wonder how to find out about all the latest Berkley Prime Crime and Signet mysteries?

berkleysignetmysteries.com

- *See what's new*
- *Find author appearances*
- *Win fantastic prizes*
- *Get reading recommendations*
- *Sign up for the mystery newsletter*
- *Chat with authors and other fans*
- *Read*

MYSTERY SOLVED.

...eries.com